T0049551

TALES OF ENLIGHTENMENT

TALES OF ENLIGHTENMENT

Stories from an era of great exploration...

This volume features original fiction set 150 years before the induction and destruction of Starlight Beacon. Journey back to a time of limitless promise and grand opportunity, as Jedi and Pathfinder teams look to discover hyperlanes to open up new trade routes as the Republic expands into the Outer Rim. However, danger lurks in every corner of the galaxy...

On the moon of Jedha stands Enlightenment, a tapbar located in the heart of the Holy City. This collection contains five short stories from the pages of *Star Wars Insider*, as told from the perspective of patrons and visitors to the establishment, as well as the exclusive tale, "Missing Pieces."

Additionally, authors new to *The High Republic*, Zoraida Córdova, Tessa Gratton, Lydia Kang, and George Mann, discuss their contributions to the books and comic stories that expand upon this exciting era of *Star Wars* storytelling.

TITAN EDITORIAL
Editor Jonathan Wilkins
Designer David Colderley
Group Editor Jake Devine
Editorial Assistant Ibraheem Kazi
Art Director Oz Browne
Production Manager Jackie Flook
Production Controller Kelly Fenlon & Caterina Falqui
Sales & Circulation Manager Steve Tothill
Marketing & Advertisement Assistant Lauren Noding
Publicist Caitlin Storer
Publishing Director Ricky Claydon
Publishing Director John Dziewiatkowski
Executive Vice President Andrew Sumner
Publishers Vivian Cheung & Nick Landau
Special Thanks: Christopher Cooper

DISTRIBUTION
U.S. Distribution: Penguin Random House
U.K. Distribution: MacMillan Distribution
Direct Sales Market: Diamond Comic Distributors
General Inquires: customerservice@titanpublishingusa.com

Star Wars: The High Republic: Tales of Enlightenment is published by Titan Magazines, a division of Titan Publishing Group Limited, 144 Southwark Street, London, SE1 0UP
Printed in China.
For sale in the U.S., Canada, U.K., and Eire

First edition: March 2024
ISBN: 9781787741713

10 9 8 7 6 5 4 3 2 1

A CIP catalogue record for this title is available from the British Library.

Front cover illustration: Matt Allsopp
Back cover illustration: Will Htay

LUCASFILM EDITORIAL
Senior Editor Brett Rector
Art Director Troy Alders
Creative Director Michael Siglain
Story Group Leland Chee, Pablo Hidalgo, Matt Martin, Kelsey Sharpe, Emily Shkoukani, and Kate Izquiero
Creative Art Manager Phil Szostak
Asset Management Chris Argyropoulos, Gabrielle Levenson, Shahana Alam, Jackey Cabrera, Elinor De La Torre, Bryce Pinkos, Michael Trobiani, Sarah Williams
Special Thanks: Samantha Keane, Kevin Pearl, and Eugene Paraszczuk

oncept art by Andrée Wallin

Concept art by Matt Alls

CONTENTS

AUTHOR INTERVIEWS AND GUIDES

TALES OF ENLIGHTENMENT

"New Prospects"

PART ONE

By George Mann

Concept art by Matt Allsopp

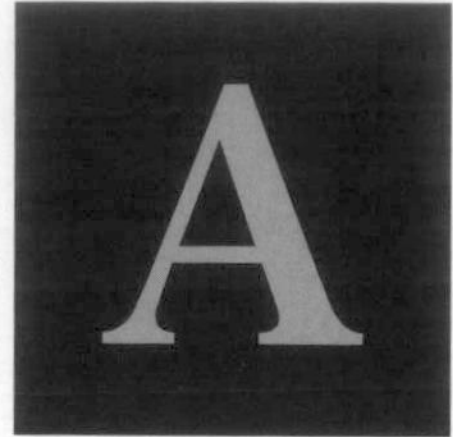

Another cold night on Jedha. Not that there was anything strange about that—every night was cold on Jedha. Cold and quiet. In fact, pretty much every day in the Holy City was the same. Keth Cerapath would wake up—inevitably late—and hurry to work in the Temple of the Kyber, where his days as an adjunct passed in silent solitude, measured out by the predictable rhythm of his chores. Day in, day out. Always the same.

It wasn't that Keth was unsatisfied with his lot—more that he longed for something to happen, just once. An interruption to the order of things. Something exciting and different; something he'd be able to talk about in years to come. The sort of story he could tell over a drink. His story. But hoping hadn't got him very far. Nothing really changed. Pilgrims came and went. The seasons turned. The preachers preached. Such was his life.

And yet, if there was one thing that Keth hoped would never change, it was Enlightenment. The tapbar was down a quiet side street, close to the markets, with a big red double door emblazoned with its name in aurebesh. Enlightenment was anything but demure. And that was what Keth liked best about it.

He nodded to the two all but identical, towering figures at the door as he strode in. "Camille. Delphine. Looking wonderful tonight as always."

Enlightenment's duo of immense Gloovan bodyguards—The Twinkle Sisters—stared back at him blankly but stood aside to allow him to pass all the same. He hurried down the steps.

On the stage, Madelina, the electro-harpist, was attacking the instrument with her usual aplomb. Keth supposed her music was meant to be soothing, but in truth it was as bemusing and impenetrable as the Iktotchi herself. Still, familiarity had bred a certain fondness, and he often found himself humming her strange, looping compositions as he went about his day.

He crossed to the bar, where Kradon, the Villarandi owner of Enlightenment—with his large, segmented body and multiple, insectoid limbs—appeared to be deep in conversation with a human woman that Keth had never seen. Keth presumed they were engaged in some business transaction or other. Enlightenment had always been a haven for any and all people, from right across the galaxy, no matter their religion, species or creed. Neutral territory. A place where you checked your issues and aggravations at the door. But that also meant that Kradon got to talk with a lot of interesting people, and he wasn't beyond passing on what he knew for the right price. In fact, he'd become the go-to person on Jedha for anyone who needed, well, pretty much anything.

Rather than disturb them—it never paid to disturb Kradon—Keth sought out his usual seat at the bar, where Piralli, a Sullustan dock worker, and Moona, a green-skinned Twi'lek who never seemed to leave the place, were already bickering over some hypothetical, most-likely ridiculous situation. It was their favorite pastime.

"Hey, kid," said Moona, raising her glass in acknowledgment as Keth slid onto his stool. "You're late."

Keth shrugged. "Peethree needed a bit of fine tuning." P3-7A was Keth's droid, saved from scrap and rebuilt by Bonbraks, who had given it the vocoder from an old Temple droid that had been decommissioned by Keth's employers. As such it could only speak in epithets derived from the other droid's limited vocab database, and had a reputation for being a little pious, despite the fact Keth knew most of what it said was its frustrated attempts at searing sarcasm. It had been barred from Enlightenment soon after its first visit.

"You'd be better off scrapping that thing," said Piralli. "More trouble than it's worth."

"Every night," said Keth, rolling his eyes. "You got nothing better to worry about than my droid?"

"Hey, I'm just looking out for a friend. No harm in that, is there?"

"You ignore him, kid," said Moona. "He's only jealous."

"Jealous? I can get myself beat up easy enough. I don't need no droid to rile up the locals for me."

"Enlightenment had always been a haven for any and all people, from right across the galaxy, no matter their religion, species or creed. Neutral territory."

"Never a truer word said," muttered Moona under her breath.

Keth nodded to old Chantho, the Ithorian barkeep.

"What you having, Keth?" The Ithorian's voice buzzed from a small box around his throat.

"I'll take a retsa."

"Tough day?"

Keth shrugged. "Same old, same old." He glanced back at the woman talking to Kradon. "Who's the newcomer?"

Piralli took a swig from his glass of blue mappa, and then leaned forward in his seat, lowering his voice conspiratorially. "Prospector. Washed up here after a job went wrong. Kradon's wringing her for information."

Keth eyed the woman for a moment longer, then turned back to the others. "Busy tonight." He could see a table of Dagoyan masters huddled in one of the alcoves, and a lone, robed figure wearing a skull mask that could only be one of the Brothers of the Ninth Door, a local, secretive sect. Other tables were overflowing with pilgrims, tourists and locals, their voices raised in a mix of merriment and healthy debate.

"Hmmm," said Piralli. "It's only going to get worse, too, with that festival the Convocation's planning. Soon we won't be able to move in here for tourists."

"All good for business, yes?" came a reedy voice from over Keth's shoulder. "But worry not, my friends. Kradon will always ensure the seats remain empty for his favorites."

Keth turned to see Kradon—and the prospector woman—standing behind him. "Oh, hey, Kradon."

"Keth, my boy! It is good to see you." Kradon angled his rippling body to indicate the woman by his side. "Here, meet Kradon's new acquaintance, Saretha von Beel. She is a hyperspace prospector in need of work."

"And a drink," added the woman. Her accent was thick and unfamiliar. She was tall and muscular, with dark brown skin and blonde hair.

"But, alas, all of her credits were lost during a terrible incident. Kradon is most sad to consider her poor situation."

Keth glanced at Piralli and Moona. Then back at the woman. "You have somewhere to stay? I work at the Temple of the Kyber. I could speak with one of the disciples…?"

Saretha shook her head. "No, thank you. I still have my ship, although she's in a sorry state. She's in for repairs, while I try to find some way to pay for them."

"What happened to you?" asked Moona.

"Oh, you know. Pirates. Jedi. Monsters." Saretha smiled.

"Jedi?" said Keth, trying to keep the reverence out of his voice.

"Yeah, but it's a long story," the prospector shrugged.

"We've got time," said Keth, settling back on his stool.

"All right. I know. How about I'll tell you my story for the price of a drink?" She cocked a smile.

Keth glanced at the others, then shot her a smile of his own. "Okay, deal." He turned to old Chantho. "I'll get this. Whatever she wants." He narrowed his eyes as he looked back at the grinning prospector. "Within reason."

"Oh, I don't have expensive tastes. A retsa will do nicely."

Keth breathed a little sigh of relief. He gestured to a stool. Saretha sat, while old Chantho poured her a ▸

suspiciously generous-looking measure of retsa.

The prospector eyed the glass with appreciation. "Oh, I've been waiting for this." She picked it up, tipped her head back and downed the entire contents of the glass in one deft movement. The empty glass hit the bar with a klink. Saretha sighed. "That's better."

Piralli gave a short, sharp burst of laughter. "Oh, I like her," he said, reaching for his own drink.

"So—this story," prompted Moona.

Saretha wiped her mouth with the back of her hand. "Have any of you ever been to Batuu?" She studied their blank expressions. "I'll take that as a no. Well, I'd been working in the Outer Rim, using Black Spire Outpost as a base."

"Scoping out new hyperspace routes?" asked Keth.

"Trying to. But the routes around Batuu are all pretty much mapped, so I was pushing out further and further into the Frontier. Of course, that brings bigger rewards… *if* you can find the passage. But it also brings bigger risks."

"Pirates," said Moona.

Saretha nodded. "Pirates. And particularly ugly ones at that." She rapped her fingertips on the bar. "I'd just emerged from a new route. Not an especially useful one, but I'd mapped it all the same, ready to register. The pirates were waiting for me when I'd completed my jump."

"They we're expecting you?" said Piralli.

Saretha shrugged. "Perhaps. They could have tracked me from Batuu. Or someone might have sold me out. Either way, I stood no chance. They clamped me with a tractor beam and blew the airlock. I managed to take a Neimoidian down with a hypowrench, but the others were too quick. They knocked me out with a stun baton and dragged me onto their ship while they pillaged everything I owned."

"I'm sorry," said Keth. "But you must have escaped? If you're here, I mean?"

"Whoa! Who's getting ahead of himself?"

"Sorry," said Keth, a little sheepishly. "Go on."

"When I came round, I was lying in a cell. It was dark and dank, and there was nothing but a dirty old cot and a bucket in the corner. My head was on fire, and I remember groaning as I tried to sit up. That was when I first saw him."

"Who?"

"The Jedi."

Keth took another sip of his drink. This was getting good. He'd seen Jedi before, of course, here on Jedha. But he'd never actually spoken to one. He'd always wanted to, but the time had never quite seemed right.

"He was just sitting there on the floor of the next cell, his legs crossed, his hands resting on his knees," Saretha went on. "His eyes were closed, and he looked like he was asleep. But he must have noticed me looking, because he sighed loudly, and without turning his head, he said 'This is unfortunate.'

"'Unfortunate isn't the word', I said. 'Everything I own is on that ship.' And that's when he opened his big, brown eyes, turned his head to look at me and said 'Ownership is merely a transitory state in the temporal existence of an object. Most 'things' will outlive their

Something clattered against the bars of his cell. And then it was in his hand, and his lightsaber was igniting with the brightest blue glow I'd ever seen.

original custodians several lifetimes over. It is a useful perspective. Freeing.'"

"Heh. Sounds like your droid, Keth," said Piralli.

"If you've ever met Master Lee Harro, you'd know that he doesn't say much, but when he does, he never knowingly uses one word when three would do. And I'm sure when that man dreams, it's of star charts and ancient, forgotten languages. He exudes knowledge from his very pores. But right there and then, in that cell, he was grumpy," said Saretha.

"Well, I'd be pretty grumpy too, if I found myself stuck in a dingy cell on a pirate ship," said Piralli.

"But that's just it. Master Harro wasn't grumpy because he was stuck in a cell. He was grumpy because he was going to have to get out of it."

"That doesn't make sense," said Moona.

"Very little about that man makes sense," said Saretha.

"So, what happened?" said Keth.

"'I suppose you'll be wanting your ship back,' said the Jedi, with a big sigh. And then he slowly got to his feet, rolled his shoulders, and reached out his hand. Something clattered against the bars of his cell. And then it was in his hand, and his lightsaber was igniting with the brightest blue glow I'd ever seen.

"He nodded at me, just once, and then slashed the bars at the front of his cell, cutting his way out in three short strokes of his shimmering blade. He made straight for the exit. I shouted after him—wasn't he going to free me, too? But he just ignored my plea and strolled off as if he didn't have a care in the world."

"I can't believe a Jedi would leave you stranded like that," said Keth.

"I can," muttered Moona.

"Ten minutes later he was back," said Saretha. "Somehow, he'd managed to round up every single pirate—the entire crew—and lock them in the hold. He opened my own cell with a flick of his laser sword and showed me back to my ship. Of course, they'd already been through all my stuff, but I just wanted to get out of there as fast as I could."

"But here's the thing I don't understand," said Keth. "The Jedi could have done that at any point, if all it took was a Force trick to get his lightsaber back. He could have been free any time he wanted."

"Exactly," said Saretha. "He'd chosen not to."

"But why?"

"Because it turns out—*he'd got himself caught on purpose*." Saretha laughed. "Not because he was trying to infiltrate the pirates or anything, you understand, but because they were headed in the right direction for him, and he wanted a ride."

"He what?" said Piralli.

Saretha nodded. "I know how it sounds, but that's the sort of man Lee Harro is. There was this planet he wanted to reach, deep in the Outer Rim. A place called Vexos. Something to do with his research. It seems the pirates were going that way. Harro had lost his own ship after some incident with a gravity sink on the planet Chardis. So, he 'got in the way' of the pirates on Batuu and got himself locked in their cell for the duration of the trip. Until I turned up, of course, and he felt obliged to help me."

"That's the Jedi way," said Keth.

"What happened next?" asked Moona.

"I felt responsible, of course. If he hadn't helped me, he'd have still been on his way to Vexos. And it seemed important to him. So, once we'd disentangled ourselves from the pirate ship, I offered to drop him off. Little did I know the place was going to be seething with enormous monsters... or that Master Harro was soon going to get us eaten by one of them."

"Eaten!" said Keth, trying to keep the disbelief out of his voice.

"Now you're just tugging my lekku," added Moona.

"You heard me," said Saretha. "Eaten." She folded her arms across her chest as if that was the end of the story.

"But... how?"

Saretha offered Keth a beaming smile. "Ah, well, if you want to know the rest, you'll have to stump up for another drink. All this talking is thirsty work."

Keth heaved a huge sigh of mock surrender and gestured for old Chantho to top up her glass. Then he settled back in his seat and took another swig of his own retsa, sighing with satisfaction. The night was looking up.

TO BE CONTINUED...

TALES OF ENLIGHTENMENT

"New Prospects"

PART TWO

By George Mann

Concept art by Will Htay

Previously, in a galaxy far, far away....

A prospector taking refreshment at the Enlightenment cantina regales the regulars with a tale of a deadly encounter with space pirates, a mysterious Jedi, and being eaten by a monster.

Somewhat inebriated from the amount of blue mappa he'd consumed, Piralli blurted out, "What you are saying doesn't make any *sense*. You can't be *eaten* by a monster and then live to tell the tale."

Saretha von Beel fixed him with a wry smile and reached for her own freshly charged glass of retsa. "And you know this because *you've* been up close and personal with a monster's insides before?"

"Well, no. Of course not," retorted Piralli. "That's kind of my point." He shrugged and glanced to Keth as if looking for support, but Keth could tell from the big grin the Sullustan was wearing that he was as taken in by Saretha's tale as the rest of them.

The prospector nodded. "Well, then. Allow me to enlighten you. But I'd better warn you—it's not for the faint hearted."

"Kradon finds none of the best tales are." Keth turned in his stool to see the Villarandi owner of Enlightenment had surreptitiously found himself a position behind the bar, edging closer to better enjoy Saretha's story. He was making a show of wiping an empty glass, while old Chantho, the Ithorian barkeep, was busy fixing a steady flow of fresh drinks nearby.

It was busy tonight. In fact, now that Keth was paying attention, he realized that others from around the bar had abandoned their seats and begun to gather in a loose circle around Saretha, all hanging intently off the prospector's every word.

Keth shot Moona a glance and she raised her glass in salute, before knocking back the cloudy contents. Cynical as she was, even the Twi'lek was enraptured by Saretha's story.

"So, after escaping the pirates, even though they'd stolen most of your credits, you took Jedi Knight Lee Harro to the planet he'd been trying to reach?" said Keth, prompting Saretha to continue.

"That's right. A place called Vexos." She shrugged. "It seemed the right thing to do, after the guy had just saved my life and gotten me my ship back. And besides, he asked nicely."

"Probably one of those Jedi mind tricks," said Moona, waving her hand before her face, "forcing you to do stuff you didn't really want to do."

Saretha laughed. "Harro isn't like that. I knew what I was doing. But I had no idea what I was getting myself into." She took a swig of her drink. "I guess I'd imagined there'd be some sort of settlement. A city, maybe. An outpost. But Vexos was just an uninhabited wilderness. Completely empty."

She glanced at her glass as if to underline her words, and then placed it on the bar. Old Chantho reached over and refilled it, as if on reflex.

"We touched down on a large, jagged outcropping of black rock, so slick and shiny you'd have thought it was glass. The whole place was covered in these immense stone cliffs, like spines emerging from the back of some gigantic beast. Not a glimpse of civilization in sight—no buildings, ships, campsites... No habitation of any kind. The air outside was thick and rancid with the smell of decaying vegetation, drifting up from the steaming valleys below."

"What did a Jedi want with a place like that?" said Piralli.

"Maybe he was looking for an old Jedi temple?" ventured Keth.

Saretha shot him an impressed look. "Not quite. But you're close. Harro told me there'd once been a sect of Force-users who'd lived on Vexos, millennia ago. Or so his research had led him to believe. He was there to see if any trace of them still existed."

"And you decided to stick around," said Moona, "just in case there was a profit to be turned?"

Saretha nodded, unashamed. "Like I said, I'd lost everything but my ship. If there were relics on Vexos that could help me recover some of what I'd lost—well, it seemed like fate. And besides, when I'd agreed to take Harro there, I'd assumed there'd be some sort of

"Handy thing about having a Jedi around—they've got a built-in early warning system."

inhabited outpost or station. But given the place was a complete wilderness, I figured I couldn't just leave him stranded there, with no way off world again."

"So, you went with him to explore?" said Keth.

"*Explore* might be too strong a word for it," said Saretha. "Harro seemed to know exactly where he was going. He led us down into one of the gullies, and from there, deeper into the wilderness below. It was dark and overgrown. The vegetation was thick and pervasive, and even the rocks were covered in a deep, purple moss. We used ropey vines to swing even lower, to where a fast-flowing river slashed through the base of the valley. It was raining, but we were sheltered by a canopy of leaves and branches that clung to the cliff walls." She rubbed the back of her neck, her expression pained. "It was a perfect hunting ground."

"So, *this* is when you got eaten?" murmured Keth, wide-eyed.

"Nope. This is when we *nearly* got eaten. When the strostodons came for us."

"What the hell is a strostathon?" bungled Piralli.

"Something you never, *ever* want to meet," said Saretha. "A giant bird, about three meters tall, that walks on two legs and has a beak that could take your head off in one snap."

Moona blew a long, low whistle. "I don't envy you, facing off against one of those things."

Saretha shook her head. "Oh, no. Not *one*. They hunt in *packs*."

Keth shuddered.

"Harro was poking around in the undergrowth," Saretha continued, "looking for the entrance to an old cave system—or so I realized later. Like I said, he rarely spoke, so it was something of a surprise when he told me to 'edge back slowly without making any sudden movements'".

"He'd sensed them coming, hadn't he? He knew you were in danger," said Keth.

Saretha nodded. "Handy thing about having a Jedi around—they've got a built-in early warning system." She pushed her stool back and got to her feet, smoothing the front of her tunic. "But in this case, it wasn't early enough. The strostodons burst out of the tree cover. Five, maybe six of them. Screeching so loud I swear you could have heard them on Coruscant."

Piralli was leaning forward on his stool. "What did you do?"

Saretha cocked a smile. "I didn't even have a blaster, not after the pirates had taken all my stuff. I just grabbed one of the hanging vines and started climbing. *Quickly*." She frowned, as if recalling something unpleasant. "Now, like I said, these creatures were *big*, and while they couldn't fly, they *could* jump and glide." She reached down, rolling up the leg of her coveralls. Keth looked down in astonishment at the lurid pink scar that curled around the base of her calf. "One of them caught me by the leg as I tried to swing into the trees for cover."

"Ouch," said Moona.

Saretha nodded. "I thought I was going to lose my leg. Probably bleed to death there and then in the bottom of that stinking valley. But that's when Harro did his Jedi thing."

"He used his lightsaber?"

Saretha shook her head. "No. He hadn't even *drawn* that. He just stood there as the creatures converged on him, eyes closed, hands outstretched. For a moment I thought he'd simply reconciled himself to death, but then something weird happened."

"What?" said Moona.

"The strostodons just *stopped*."

"Stopped?" echoed Keth.

Saretha nodded. "They just hung their heads and began making trilling sounds. As if they were placid, peaceful creatures that had never had any intention of eating us."

"The wound on your leg suggests otherwise," said Piralli.

"It does, at that," agreed Saretha. "Harro told me later that he'd reached out through the Force to commune ▸

with them. To help them to see us as friends, rather than food." She rolled her trouser leg back down over her boot. "I only wish he'd done it a bit sooner."

"*See*," said Moona, wagging her finger. "Jedi mind tricks."

"I suppose it was, in a way," said Saretha. "But however he did it, I was grateful to Harro. He'd saved my life. *Again.*"

"So, the strostodons just… *left*?" asked Keth.

"Yes and no," said Saretha. "You see, it turns out Vexos was a pretty hostile place, and they weren't the only predators down there in the gully. Harro had pacified the strostodons, and with a flick of his wrist, he sent the entire pack on its way. As we watched them thunder off through the undergrowth, though, that's when the *real* danger presented itself."

"So, *this* is when you got eaten?" said Piralli.

"I'm getting there," said Saretha, rolling her eyes. "There was a massive rumbling sound, and then the ground nearby just *erupted*. The head of an immense worm burst out from the undergrowth, its pale flesh rippling as its fanged maw gaped wide. It grabbed one of the trailing strostodons and *swallowed* it whole. Then it simply slithered back into whatever 'home' it had crept from, disappearing almost as quickly as it had arrived.

"I stood there, speechless and trembling. And that was when Harro walked over to stand beside me. 'Ah,' he said, with a broad grin. 'Looks like we've found the way into the caves.'"

"What about your leg?" asked Keth.

"Harro helped me bind it. Thankfully the wound wasn't too severe, although I wasn't going to be running anywhere for a while. He explained that the worm was a parasite, one of dozens of them down there in the valley, that had taken up residence in the cave tunnels, blocking the way in and out of the underground warren. And of course, the warren was exactly where he wanted to go."

"So, you had to kill one of the worms, right?" offered Piralli.

Saretha shook her head. "Harro is a *Jedi*. The idea of killing an innocent creature was anathema to him. No, his plan was far worse. He planned to encourage the worm to eat us."

"That's insane!" said Piralli.

"Exactly what I said," agreed Saretha. "But Harro was adamant. The best way down to the caves was to allow the worm to swallow us. You see, the worm was just one appendage of a much larger creature, like an esophagus leading down to the stomach below. Harro's plan was to use it like a tunnel—to let it swallow us, and then find a way to avoid the pools of digestive acid awaiting us below, before exiting through the, well, you know…"

"In the name of the Force," muttered Keth.

Saretha shrugged. "I have to hand it to him—it worked. I'll spare you the worst of the details, but when that fleshy throat closed around our bodies and dragged us in… let's just say I'm still not sure I've got the stink out of my hair. The slime…" She pulled a face. "The muscles rippled and propelled us down the chute of its throat at some speed.

"Thankfully, Harro was able to slow our descent with the Force, and we narrowly avoided the rancid pools of stomach juice, where our friend the strostodon was already in the process of being digested."

Beside him, Keth noticed Piralli shudder.

"It was then that I realized several other worm-like throats all led down to the same place. It was as if the creature had grown *inside* the rock, filling the available space. We skirted around the

"There was a massive rumbling sound, and then the ground nearby just erupted. The head of an immense worm burst out of the undergrowth."

acid, along another stinking tunnel where the walls quivered nervously at our presence, and eventually found our way out of the thing's insides."

"Into the cave system?" said Keth.

Saretha nodded. "Harro was delighted, of course. Personally, I couldn't see what all the fuss was about. The caves showed signs that they had once been inhabited—a few primitive paintings smeared on the walls, the remains of a bunch of old pots, and a small chunk of rock that Harro seemed particularly enamored with. He told me that he was on a quest, like Barnabus Vim and others of his Order, venturing out into the frontier to search for new ways to learn about the Force. Although, if truth be told, I had no idea what *anyone* could learn from a few musty old caves like that. We were down there for a couple of hours while he recorded his findings before he finally managed to find us another way out. This time, via an old set of carved steps in the rock, because I swore that there was no way I was venturing back the same way we'd come.

"We emerged into the light, covered in mucus and other unmentionable dirt, only to find there was someone waiting for us, blasters held at the ready."

"The pirates!" Blurted Keth, on the edge of his stool.

"They'd followed us to Vexos, looking for revenge on Harro for ruining their haul."

"What did you do?" gasped Moona.

"Me? Oh, I just put up my hands, closed my eyes, waiting for the inevitable," Saretha laughed. "Some people never learn, me included."

She took another sip of her drink, leaving her audience hanging.

"And...?!" Piralli demanded, impatiently.

"Harro whistled," Saretha smiled. "And a moment later, that flock of strostodons burst out of the undergrowth. Those pirates didn't know which way to turn."

"What happened to them?" said Keth, scandalized.

"They took off, in every direction. If they didn't end up as worm food, they're probably still there now," Saretha shrugged. "Harro took their ship, headed off to continue his explorations elsewhere on the frontier, and I had just enough fuel to make it here, to Jedha." She pulled a fist-sized hunk of rock from her pocket and tossed it in the air, before catching it again. It seemed to sparkle as it caught the low lights of the bar.

"Harro gave me the hunk of rock he'd found in the caves as a souvenir." She grinned. "I hope I'll run into him again someday, but somehow I doubt it. People like Lee Harro—they're a once-in-a-lifetime sort of encounter."

"So, now you're stranded here on Jedha, until you can figure out how to pay for repairs and fuel," said Piralli.

"That's about the size of it," said Saretha. "Although it doesn't seem like such a bad place."

"Can I take a look at that rock?" said Keth.

"Sure." Saretha tossed it over to him with a quizzical expression. "Although it's nothing special. I figured I'd mount it in my cockpit, as a reminder of Harro."

Keth turned the rock over in his hands. A broad smile crept onto his face. "This is pure kyber," he said, holding the rock up so it caught the light. "It's worth a small fortune."

"It is?" said Saretha.

"This'll more than pay for your repairs," said Keth. "And Jedha is just the place to sell it, too. I can show you where."

Saretha reached over and took the rock back from Keth, regarding it in a new light as she weighed it up in her hand. "The old dog. He knew exactly what he was giving me, didn't he?"

Keth laughed. "I guess he did."

Saretha patted Keth on the shoulder. "Thanks for the drinks, kid," she said, as she returned to her stool. Behind her, the small audience was peeling away as the other patrons went back to their own seats.

"Well, seems you *can* survive being eaten by a monster," said Piralli.

"And being kidnapped by a Jedi," said Moona.

Keth shook his head. "It was a good story. Thank you."

Saretha tossed the hunk of kyber into the air, catching it again in one hand. She turned back to Keth, Piralli and Moona, and smiled. "Well, friends," she said. "Looks like the next round's on me."

THE END.

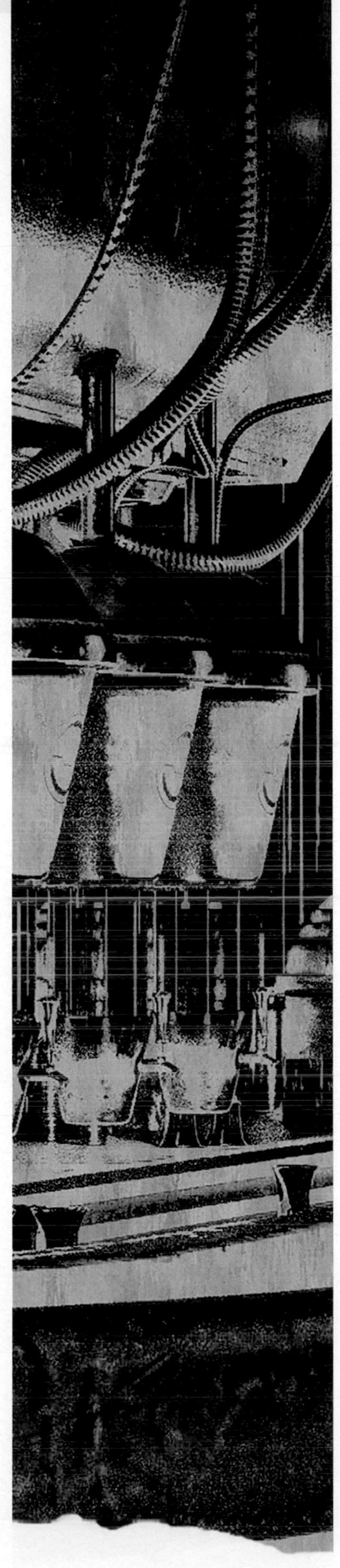

STAR WARS
THE HIGH REPUBLIC

TALES OF ENLIGHTENMENT

"A Different Perspective"

By George Mann

Concept art by Matt Allsopp

he afternoon light was beginning to wane as Keth made his way through the still-bustling markets of Jedha. A cold wind was blowing in off the desert, stirring fingers of sand that clawed at the high walls of the city. People jostled and milled amongst the busy stalls, feigning politeness as they muttered veiled curses beneath their breaths. Preparations were underway for the inaugural Festival of Balance, the new celebration of the Force that had been instigated by the Convocation as a means of bringing various Force sects together and inspiring a culture of compromise and collaboration. At least, that was the intention.

The result was that there'd been a recent influx of tourists, pilgrims, and adherents to the aforementioned sects, which in turn meant the city was busier than Keth had ever seen it, and tensions were riding high. Protest groups were making regular processions through the city streets. He could hear one now—the so-called 'Path of the Open Hand'—loudly preaching that 'the Force will be free!' as they marched by in a column, robes swishing with every proclamation.

Not only that, but in the past few days delegations had begun to arrive from the worlds of Eiram and E'ronoh, twin planets that had been locked in a bitter war for more than five years. Their ambassadors were now coming to the supposed 'neutral ground' of Jedha to settle their differences and sign a peace treaty, following a well-publicized marriage between the heirs of both worlds. The Elders of the Church of the Force had been growing increasingly agitated as the day of the treaty approached, and Keth's chores had increased tenfold as they hurried to prepare the Temple of the Kyber, or at least their small part of it, to receive visitors.

Still, Keth supposed the tide of newcomers also meant the street vendors were out in numbers, so there was more chance of catching something interesting for dinner. The rich, spicy scents of roasting meat and stewed vegetables made his stomach growl. He ran his fingers through his mop of dark hair and smoothed the front of his adjunct's tunic—but his efforts made little difference to his generally rumpled appearance. He always seemed to be rumpled these days.

He'd just decided to treat himself to a bowl of curried tip-yip from Old Maddia's stall—it *had* been a hard day pushing the broom around the Church halls, after all—when the sound of a backfiring speeder caused him to lurch back, just in time to see the out-of-control vehicle slide by, its panicked rider—a Togruta—fighting desperately to prevent the machine from hurtling at speed towards the startled members of the nearby procession.

A scream. The whine of an engine malfunctioning. Panicked shouting.

Keth squeezed his eyes shut, expecting the worse.

The moment stretched.

And then… *silence.*

Tentatively, he opened his eyes again.

The speeder was still, hanging in mid-air, more than a meter off the ground. The Togruta, wide-eyed, was clinging to the steering wheel as if his life depended on it, breathing raggedly. Around the vehicle, the disciples of the Path of the Open Hand were falling back, hurrying away into the clamoring crowds. Within a moment, they'd all disappeared.

Before the speeder stood a lone figure in brown and white robes. Her hand was raised towards the vehicle, and she was wearing a look of fierce concentration. She was human, with pale skin and red and white streaked hair, and looked to be no older than Keth. A metal cylinder hung from a holster at her belt.

A lightsaber.

The woman was a *Jedi.*

Slowly, she lowered her outstretched hand and the speeder followed in kind, lowering to a safely static hover. The driver clambered off, trembling, and looking around in astonishment. There was a muted round of applause from the crowd. The Jedi grinned.

It was only then that Keth noticed the person sprawled on the ground. It was one of the Path disciples—a male Abednedo—who'd evidently tripped and fallen as he'd tried to get out of the way of the oncoming speeder and had been inadvertently left behind when the other followers of the Path had fled. As Keth watched, the Jedi crossed to the fallen disciple and held out her hand.

The disciples of the Path of the Open Hand were falling back, hurrying away.

"Are you hurt?" she said. "Let me help you up. My name is Maeve Cuilinn. I'm a—"

"No!" Rather than take the Jedi's outstretched hand, the Abednedo issued a shrill, startled cry and tried to scrabble away from the woman. Lurching awkwardly to his feet, his foot caught in his robes, he fell again, striking his head on the dusty ground. He rolled onto his side, moaning, and waving his hand violently at the Jedi to leave him alone. "No. You're a *Jedi*. Leave me be!"

The woman frowned, and then looked around, searching the faces in the crowd for an explanation. Her eyes met Keth's. He swallowed and took a step forward. "Here, let me." He hurried over to the fallen disciple.

The Abednedo was clutching his head. Keth couldn't see any signs of a serious injury, but the blow had looked painful. "No! Leave me!"

"It's all right. I'm here to help."

"Are you with the Jedi?"

Keth frowned. "No."

The Abednedo heaved a sigh of relief. "Then help me get away from here. As quickly as possible. Please." The last word was spoken with such intensity that Keth knew he had no choice but to help.

"Yes. Of course." Keth turned to look up at the Jedi. "I think you'd better leave this to me."

The Jedi gave a slow, uncertain nod, and then began to back away, evidently aware that her presence was causing the fallen disciple's distress. Keth helped the Abednedo unsteadily to his feet. He wavered a little, and clasped Keth's shoulder to right himself.

Keth held him firm. "Come on. I know a place nearby where we can go."

Inside Enlightenment, it was quieter than normal, although Madelina was on the stage as usual, stirring some sad lament from her electro-harp. A few scattered patrons nursed drinks by the bar or sat quietly at tables, minding their own business. There was no sign of either Piralli or Moona.

Keth showed the Abednedo to a booth in a quiet corner. He didn't seem to have any obvious injuries beyond the nasty blow he'd taken to the back of his head, and he already seemed to be regaining his senses and coordination. He also seemed much less agitated now that they'd put some distance between themselves and the Jedi woman who'd saved him in the market.

Keth was just about to ask the Abednedo his name, when he heard scuttling feet approaching from across the bar. He stifled a grin. "Hello, Kradon." The Villarandi had never been able to resist interpolating himself into a conversation—especially if it involved a newcomer to the bar.

Kradon smiled broadly as he approached the booth. "Kradon sees you have a new friend, Keth! Most welcome. Most welcome!" He turned to address the Abednedo. "This is your first time patronizing Enlightenment, is it not…?"

"Whool," said the Abednedo. "My name is Whool."

"Whool," repeated Kradon. He made a sort of whistling sound as he formed the word. "What can Kradon offer you on this most fortuitous day?"

"Fortuitus?" Whool frowned.

"Why, yes!" said Kradon. "Fortuitus because you are here! All are welcome here in Enlightenment!"

Whool nodded appreciatively, and then winced and touched a hand against the back of his head. "I'll just have a glass of water, please."

"You will?"

"Whool had an… accident in the market. He banged his head," said Keth.

"Then Kradon shall fetch your water immediately. And a retsa for Keth, of course! All on the tab." He scuttled off towards the bar.

Keth watched him go, then turned to Whool. "How are you feeling?"

Whool seemed to consider this for a moment. "I'm all right. A little woozy and sore. Thank you for your assistance."

"You're welcome," said Keth. ▸

"But…" he hesitated for a moment, and then decided he wouldn't be able to rest until he'd asked the question. "That Jedi—she was trying to help you. You seemed so afraid. What happened?"

Whool looked uncomfortable. "She used the Force to save my life, preventing the speeder from running me down." He folded his hands on his lap, as if to stop himself from fidgeting.

"But surely that's a *good* thing?" offered a perplexed Keth.

Whool's head snapped up, and for the first time since they'd arrived at the bar, he met Keth's eye, fixing him with an intense stare. "No. It's *not.* Not at all."

"But…" Keth trailed off, frowning. Did the Abednedo have some sort of death wish? "You might have been killed."

Whool issued a circumspect sigh. "If such was the will of the Force, who am I to wish otherwise?"

"Then you believe in *destiny*?" said Keth. "That everything is predetermined by the Force?"

Whool shook his head. "No. I—we of the Path—believe that the Force flows freely, and its currents are not to be disturbed. What the Jedi did, manipulating the Force like that, will have dire consequences."

"But the Jedi do that all the time."

"Precisely!" said Whool. All thoughts of his sore head now seemed to be forgotten. He leaned across the table. "Every day, the Jedi abuse the sanctity of the living Force. They twist it for their own ends. But the Force must find balance. If a life is saved *here,*" Whool held up his left hand, cupped into a loose fist, "then another will be taken *here.*" He gestured with his right hand.

Keth rubbed his chin, feeling uncomfortable. He wished Kradon would hurry back with the drinks. "But that's not what they teach us at the Church. The Jedi *commune* with the Force. They help people."

"So they think," said Whool. "But they do not understand the consequences of their actions. They are too quick to swoop in and save the day. They bend the Force to their will, and then are gone before they're made to witness the aftermath of their actions. This is what the Path of the Open Hand has come to Jedha to teach. The Force *must* be allowed to flow freely. The Jedi, and all those like them who manipulate the Force, must be stopped."

So *that* was what all the chanting and processions were about. The Path of the Open Hand hadn't been on Jedha for long, and Keth had never made a point of stopping to listen to their preachers. He could see now why Whool had been so afraid of the Jedi in the market—as a disciple of the Path, he seemed to truly believe that his own life had been saved at the expense of someone else's. It was a philosophy that didn't sit well with Keth. He couldn't believe the Force could be so cruel.

"Here, here, water for our guest," said Kradon, finally returning to their booth bearing a small tray. He placed the glass in front of the Abednedo, who scooped it up and thirstily drank from it. Keth sipped at his retsa, and nodded his thanks to the barkeep, who scuttled off again looking pleased with himself.

"I see that you do not agree with my words."

"It's just… it's not how I've ever understood the Force," said Keth.

"You're not unusual in that," said Whool. "If you would humor me just a short while longer, perhaps you'd allow me to tell you the story of my brother, Grael."

Keth nodded. "Of course."

Whool set his now-empty glass on the table. "I grew up amongst a family of miners. My mother had been a miner, and her father before her. We sought the adelyne crystals that are buried deep in the crust of our planet—the resource that has helped to make our world rich. Yet, after generations of exploitation, we were forced to dig deeper into the cave

"There were ten of us drilling out a new seam. But we didn't know the seam was unstable. I drilled too deep and…"

systems beneath the surface to seek less and less accessible seams.

"Now, Grael had always been something of a strange child. He didn't play well with others and was shy and retiring, unlike his more gregarious older sibling." Whool tapped his chest and offered a wan smile. "We'd always known he was different. But as he grew, he began to exhibit certain… abilities. Or rather, strange things began to happen around him whenever he grew anxious, angry, or confused."

"He was Force sensitive," said Keth.

"Quite so. But my parents, fearing we would lose him to the Jedi who regularly visited our world to steal away such Force-sensitive children, helped him learn to suppress his unwanted emergent powers."

"So, he buried them away, closing himself off to the Force?" said Keth.

"He learned self-control," said Whool. "Back then, I had yet to come to the teachings of the Path of the Open Hand, but we all knew instinctively that Grael's so-called powers were *wrong*. And so yes, he buried them, and we never spoke of it again. Life went on as before, and we both trained to follow in our mother's footsteps and work the mines, as had always been our destiny. Or so we thought." Whool drummed his fingers on the tabletop.

"Something went wrong," said Keth.

"It was late one night. Grael and I were working the same shift, deep down in the mines. There were ten of us drilling out a new seam. But we didn't know the seam was unstable. I drilled too deep and…"

"The mine collapsed."

Whool nodded. "The cavern ceiling gave way. We would all have been crushed—if it wasn't for Grael, who, in his fear and desperation, reached for the Force."

"He held back the collapsing rocks?" asked Keth.

"He did. Long enough for us all to escape. All ten of us made it out alive, and for the first time, I began to doubt what my parents had done to my brother. Me and the other miners—we celebrated Grael that night. We were alive because of him. Why shouldn't he revel in his power? Why *shouldn't* he use it for good?" Whool sighed, caught up in the memory. "But the next morning we got our answer. While we'd been celebrating our own good fortune, another mine had collapsed. One that should have been stable. More than thirty people were crushed to death."

"But that happens in mines all of the time," said Keth. "It wasn't your fault. Or Grael's. It's just a tragic accident."

Whool shook his head. "*No.* It was the Force seeking balance. Can't you see that? If we'd died in that cavern as we were meant to, those other people would have survived."

"And you think the same is true of what happened today, in the market?" said Keth. "You think that because that Jedi saved your life, someone else will die."

"I don't think it. I *know* it," said Whool. He stood, smoothing the front of his robes. "I can see that you will not be convinced. But please, all I ask is that you think on what I've said."

Keth nodded. "Are you sure you're okay?"

"I am quite well. I shall return to my people. Thank you for your assistance." He gave a brief bow, and then turned and strode from the bar. On his way out, the Abednedo passed another person coming through the red double doors. It was Piralli.

Keth picked up his retsa and went to the bar to join the Sullustan. "Evening."

Piralli gestured for Kradon to pour him a drink. "Evening. You heard the news?"

"What news? said Keth.

"There's been a freak accident," said Piralli. "Outside the Dome of Deliverance. A speeder went haywire and crashed into a line of pilgrims. Four people are dead, including the driver."

Keth paused before his glass reached his lips. "*What?*"

"I know. Shocking, isn't it? Apparently, the same speeder nearly hit someone earlier in the market, but thankfully a Jedi was there to stop them. Shame they weren't around later, too."

Keth didn't respond.

Piralli peered at him. "Hey, are you okay?"

Keth nodded. He swallowed. And then downed his retsa in a single gulp. He glanced at the door, but there was no sign of the Abednedo. He frowned for a moment, and then shook his head, before placing his empty glass on the bar.

"You want another?" asked Piralli.

Keth shrugged. "Whatever the Force wills," he said.

THE END.

TALES OF ENLIGHTENMENT

"The Unusual Suspect"

By George Mann

Concept art by Christian Alzmann

"He's late." Piralli flicked another glance at the entrance. "What do you mean, 'he's late'?" said Moona. She placed her empty glass on the counter, motioning to Old Chantho, the Ithorian behind the bar, to top off her drink. He muttered something under his breath but splashed a refill into her glass all the same.

"Keth," said Piralli. "He's usually here by now."

"Maybe he's not coming. You know he's busy with all that peace conference stuff. It was all he was talking about yesterday, having to babysit that San Tooka guy."

"San *Tekka,*" corrected Piralli, shaking his head. "They're only the most successful hyperspace prospectors in the galaxy. Sanctioned to act as mediators for the peace talks by Chancellor Mollo himself."

"Whatever." Moona rolled her eyes. "The point stands. Keth's busy."

Piralli stared at her through the bottom of his glass. "I suppose."

"What's it matter, anyway? It's not like you to mope around after the kid."

"I want his opinion on something," said Piralli.

"Well, *there's* a twist. You're usually the first to shout him down in any argument."

Piralli sighed. "I've told you before, there's a difference between an argument and a healthy debate. It's the basis of our friendship. It's what we *do.*"

Moona nodded sarcastically. "It's what you do." She seemed taken by a sudden thought and cocked her head to one side. "Anyway, what you're saying—by implication—is that the opinion of a young human adjunct is worth more than that of a middle-aged, *experienced,* female Twi'lek."

"Who never leaves her seat at the bar," retorted Piralli, but not unkindly.

"Exactly. I see *everything* from this stool. All of life on Jedha passes through Enlightenment at one point or another. Just ask Kradon."

"I don't need to ask Kradon," said Piralli, glancing at their amiable Villerandi host, who was presently *exchanging* words with the two Gloovan bouncers he kept on staff, Camille and Delphine. Or perhaps not exchanging, exactly—the Twinkle Sisters weren't known for their verbosity.

"And I *do* value your opinion. But this falls much more in Keth's area of expertise."

Moona slid her drink off the counter and took a sip, leaning closer on her stool. Her breath smelled of retsa. "Go on. What is it?"

Piralli looked across the room towards the black-robed figure sitting in one of the nearby alcoves, alone. He was a tall, wiry, human. His hood was drawn up, casting his sallow face in deep shadow. He was sipping from what appeared to be a steaming glass of hot chea. "It's *him.* He's giving off a bad vibe."

Moona started to turn in her seat, but Piralli caught her arm. "Be subtle."

She glowered at him. "I'm *always* subtle."

"*Right,*" said Piralli, drawing out the word. "Then be *more* subtle."

With an exasperated sigh, Moona turned to regard the stranger. She looked him up and down for a moment. If he noticed her watching, he didn't show it. With another shrug, she turned back around in her seat. "You don't need Keth. *I* can tell you who he is. He's a member of one of the small Force-worshipping sects here on Jedha. The Brotherhood of the Ninth Door."

Piralli scratched his chin. "I've heard of them. Aren't they followers of the dark side?"

Moona downed the rest of her drink. "Light side, dark side, what difference does it make? They're all weirdos. Especially the Jedi."

"But it's in the name, isn't it? *Dark* side. As in dangerous. As in 'best stay out of their way'."

Moona laughed. "Light and dark are just two sides of the same coin. Day and night. Sunrise and sunset." She glanced back at the hunched figure in the alcove, and then motioned for Old Chantho to fill her empty glass again. "You worry too much. Nothing bad ever happens in Enlightenment."

That was when the doors blew open and blaster fire raked the low ceiling, sending shattered glowlamps raining to the floor.

Later, Piralli would reflect on Moona's words, and wonder whether it was all her fault for tempting fate. But at the time, it was all he could do to dive for the floor, dragging Moona off her stool behind him. They lay in a tangled heap for a moment, listening.

There was a heavy *whump* from the direction of the door. And then another. Piralli allowed himself an optimistic grin.

Whoever had come through those doors hadn't accounted for the Twinkle Sisters. He edged forward on his hands and knees, avoiding scattered shards of glass, to peer around the side of the bar.

Both Twinkle Sisters were on their backs, apparently unconscious. A rough-looking Klatooinian was detaching what appeared to be an energy weapon from Camille—a brace of small metal needles that had buried themselves in the Gloovan's flesh and still crackled with the flickering discharge of an electric current.

The bouncers had been stunned. They were out for the count. The rest of the bar's patrons were cowering in their seats or attempting to find safe places to hide, while several other heavies filed in behind the Klatooinian, all carrying blasters. They were an odd assortment of beings—a Rodian, two humans, a Frozian and an Iktotchi—all wearing matching leather waistcoats branded with the same insignia: two snake fangs dripping with venom.

A gang, then.

Piralli swallowed. This was *bad.* He edged back behind the bar, putting his finger to his lips to urge Moona to keep quiet.

"Everyone stay where you are, and we won't have to hurt you... *much,*" barked the Klatooinian, snickering at his own joke.

A ripple of silence passed through the bar.

"Now, now. Kradon would like to stress that there is no need for any *unpleasantness.* Kradon is certain that we can come to a satisfactory arrangement for us all." The Villerandi's chittering voice was as calm as ever, as if dealing with an armed invader was all just another wrinkle in a typical day's work.

"Tellion *said* you were a smooth talker," said the Klatooinian. "He also said that's what got you into this mess. *Talking too much.*"

Piralli sighed. So *that* was what this was about. Kradon had gone and upset the wrong person, probably selling information to someone unscrupulous about protecting their sources.

"Kradon does not know what you mean."

The Klatooinian answered him with another blaster shot, this time detonating a line of bottles behind the bar. "Oh, I think you know *exactly* what I mean. Tellion sends his regards. And hopes you don't mind a little mess."

Another blaster shot. Another shower of broken glass and fittings.

"And now, since we're here, we're going to make the most of it. So why don't you line up a row of your finest beverages while we liberate your patrons of their valuables."

A murmured groan passed through the bar, as the other patrons realized the true extent of their situation.

Piralli sensed movement close by and, fearing that some fool was about to try to make a break for it, was surprised to see the robed figure from earlier—the *dark sider*—had edged across the room towards an access door in the far wall, and was motioning for Piralli and Moona to follow him. Piralli glanced at Moona, half expecting to see her offering the man a rude gesture, but was even more surprised to find she was already shuffling after him, her bare knees scuffing the sticky floor.

"Wait!" hissed Piralli, but Moona just ignored him and kept on going.

Around the other side of the bar the gang members had started to force people to turn out their pockets. Kradon was doing his best to keep their Klatooinian leader talking, but just seemed to be antagonizing him further.

"Kradon can recommend far richer pickings in one of the bars on the other side of the city. They entertain *ambassadors* there..."

Another shot from the blaster, another fine vintage splashed across the floor.

Piralli glanced after Moona again, and then, with the whine of blaster fire still ringing in his ears, he hurried off after her, keeping low.

The robed figure practically shoved Piralli through the open door the moment he caught up with them. Piralli sprawled across the floor of what appeared to be a storage room off the main bar. He picked himself up, dusting himself down, just as the robed figure slipped in behind him, pushing the door shut in his wake.

The man turned to face Piralli and Moona, pulling back the cowl of his robe. His face was gaunt, and his eyes were a startling, piercing blue. "My name is Mindoku," he said. His voice had a strange warbling quality, as if three different people were speaking the same words at once, all just a fraction out of sync.

"Thank you," said Moona. "For helping us find a place to hide."

Mindoku frowned. "Hide?" He looked genuinely puzzled. "No. That's not why I called you over." ▸

"Light and dark are just two sides of the same coin. Day and night. Sunrise and sunset."

"Regardless of what you might think, I intend to help those people out there. Can I count on your assistance?"

Piralli shook his head. "Ah, here it comes. Everything has its price, right?"

Mindoku looked genuinely confused. "I don't quite follow—"

"You're going to protect us. For a *price*," said Piralli, cutting him off. "That's what this is, isn't it? You'll stop those gangsters from robbing us, but you want a cut of the proceeds yourself."

"No."

"Then *what?*"

"I require your help."

"Our help?" echoed Moona. "With what?"

"With stopping those miscreants from hurting anyone."

Piralli gaped at the man. This didn't make sense. What was his angle, here, exactly? "You're saying you want to take on the gang?"

"And that surprises you?" said Mindoku.

"It does," said Piralli. "What with you being a... well... a..."

Mindoku gave a wan smile. "I see. Well, regardless of what you might think, I intend to help those people out there. Can I count on your assistance?"

"Why do you need *our* help?" asked Moona. "Don't you have one of those laser swords, or something?"

Mindoku laughed. "As your friend is clearly so keen to remind me, I am no Jedi. And my electrostaff was confiscated by your two Gloovan friends at the door. But perhaps I can get it back, with your help."

Piralli and Moona shared a look. What choice did they have? This was Enlightenment, after all. Many of the people out there were their friends. And Piralli supposed it didn't really matter what the dark sider's agenda *really* was, so long as the result was the same—getting rid of those bandits before they did any more harm.

"All right," said Piralli. "What do you need us to do?"

"See that barrel behind you? I need you to crack it open."

Moona grinned. "Good idea. I could use a drink, and that's one of Kradon's imported Coruscant ales."

"It's not to drink," said Mindoku.

"It's not?"

Mindoku smiled. "Here's what we're going to do..."

Piralli was *certain* this was a bad idea. Any moment now, he was going to end up on the wrong end of a blaster shot, and it would all be over. He wasn't ready to die just yet. He should have stayed hidden in the storeroom.

Instead, here he was rolling a barrel of ale across Enlightenment with Moona, heading directly for the bar and the gang of armed robbers, who looked less than impressed to see them.

"Here you go, boss!" chirped Moona, brightly. "The barrel of ale you wanted." They rolled the barrel to a stop before the bar, close to where the gang members had gathered. Nearly all their blasters were now pointed in Piralli and Moona's direction.

"What is this?" spat the Klatooinian.

"A barrel of ale," said Piralli, feigning ignorance. "We were just bringing it out from the storeroom. Why, what's going on out here?" He looked at the blasters, then over to Kradon, who threw him a conspicuous wink.

"Kradon thanks you, Piralli. But I think you'd better do as our new guests say."

"Wise words," said the Klatooinian, motioning with the stub of his blaster. "Get over there and keep quiet. We'll deal with you later."

Piralli nodded as he and Moona backed away. Their feet splashed in the pool of ale that was slowly spreading from the open barrel, sloshing unnoticed around the boots of the hoodlums.

Surreptitiously, Piralli watched as Mindoku slipped from the storeroom, silently crossing the room. He neared the edge of the bar, and then... he was *gone*, and in his place stood another gangster, dressed in the same matching waistcoat as the others.

Piralli blinked and narrowed his eyes. Surely it had to be a trick of the light. But no—where Mindoku had stood was now a human gang member of around the same size and build.

The new individual walked insouciantly around the bar towards the door. The others barely paid him any notice. He stepped carefully over the supine form of Delphine and then, just as Piralli thought he was going to make a run for it, he turned left, grabbed the electrostaff that had been propped by the doorframe, and pivoted. The end of the electrostaff flickered to life. In the glow of the crackling current, Piralli glimpsed Mindoku—the real Mindoku—holding the weapon before him, his disguise now effortlessly dropped.

Mindoku plunged the electrostaff into the river of spilled ale that now sloshed around the gang members' boots, causing it to ignite with an incandescent flare. Piralli swore that the light show that had erupted was still affecting his vision three days later.

Almost as one, the twitching criminals collapsed to the floor unconscious, their blasters slipping from their limp fingers. Mindoku lifted the electrostaff, twirled it once, and killed the power.

The entire establishment seemed to draw a breath. And then a cheer erupted, as people began to cautiously emerge from their hiding places.

"Shall I send for the Guardians?" said Mindoku, turning to Kradon, who was slithering out from behind the bar, a broad grin on his face.

Kradon looked down at the prone Klatooinian. "Oh, no," he said. "Kradon has ways of dealing with such *vermin*." He clapped his hands. "But now, a drink for our honored savior, perhaps? The very least we can do. Kradon is *most* grateful for your help."

Mindoku shook his head. "No, thank you. There's no need." He glanced round as Piralli approached. "Ah, and here's my reluctant accomplice."

"What you did..." said Piralli, struggling to find the right words. "You became *someone* else."

Mindoku laughed. "That's how my relationship with the Force works. When people look at me, they see what they *want* to see. Or sometimes, what *I* want them to see."

"Most remarkable!" said Kradon.

"Hold on, doesn't that mean..." Piralli frowned. "You could have walked out of here at any point. You could have used your abilities to cloud the gang's minds and make them see you as one of their own. You could have been safe and clear away from any of this the moment it started."

Mindoku shrugged.

"But you chose not to," said Piralli. "Why?"

Mindoku offered a tight smile. "What kind of person would leave others to suffer when they knew they could help?"

"But..." started Piralli.

"But such notions don't fit with your preconceptions of people like me, do they?" finished Mindoku. "With people whose beliefs you don't understand."

"No," admitted Piralli. He felt his cheeks flush with embarrassment. "And I'm sorry."

Mindoku put a hand on Piralli's shoulder. "If it helps, just assume that I had my reasons and was getting something out of it all too." He turned and started for the door.

"But you weren't, were you? You weren't getting anything out of it," Piralli called after him. "You just wanted to help."

But Mindoku had already gone, blending seamlessly with the crowd beyond the open door.

Piralli sighed.

"I'm just sad about all that Coruscant ale," said Moona, kicking her boots through the grimy layer of ash that now covered the floor around the unconscious gangers.

"Do not worry," said Kradon, handing her a bucket and mop from beneath the bar. "Kradon will not charge you for it all at once."

Moona groaned.

She'd just started mopping the floor—while Piralli helped clear up the patina of broken glass that now seemed to cover every surface—when a boom *crack* seemed to rend the sky, causing the whole of Enlightenment to shudder.

"What the..." Piralli, frowning, stumbled towards the door and out into the sunlit street beyond, blinking in the harsh light. Others were spilling from the bar behind him, and from the surrounding buildings, too, coming out into the square and looking around, confused, for the source of the troubling sound.

Piralli felt Moona's hand on his shoulder. "There." He followed her gaze to see a huge column of oily black smoke coiling from one of the towers in the distance.

"That's the Second Spire," said Old Chantho, from behind Piralli's shoulder.

"Where they're holding the signing of the peace treaty between Eiram and E'ronoh," added Piralli.

Moona sucked in her breath. "Well, it doesn't look as though *peace* is foremost on their mind, does it?"

They stood and stared at the roiling smoke as the crowds continued to gather in the street.

"Kradon doesn't like the look of this," said the impresario, clacking his fingers against one another nervously. Behind him, the shamefaced members of the gang were slipping out of Enlightenment's doors and away into the crowd, but no one was paying them any heed. "No. Kradon doesn't like the look of this at all..."

THE END

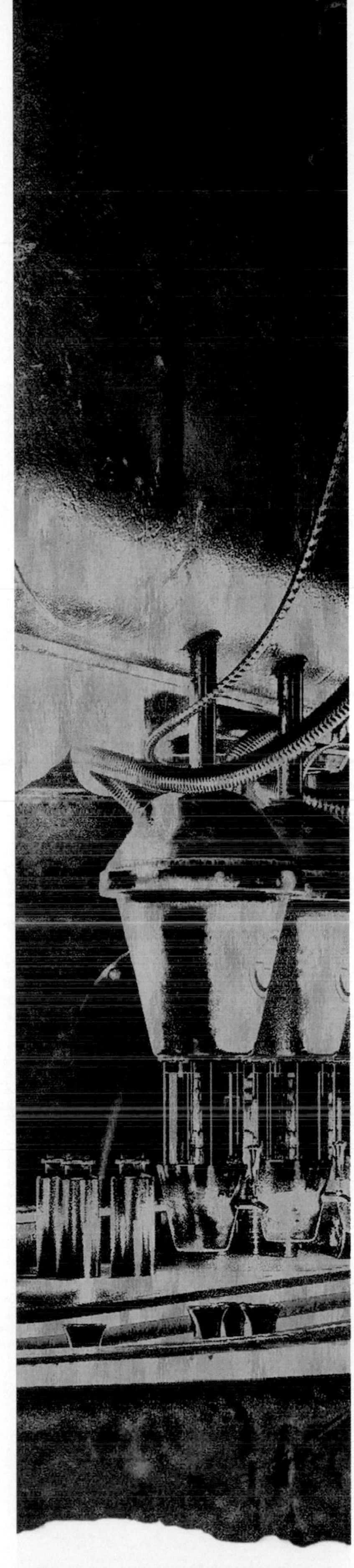

TALES OF ENLIGHTENMENT

"No Such Thing as a Bad Customer"

PART ONE

By George Mann

Concept art by Matt Allsop

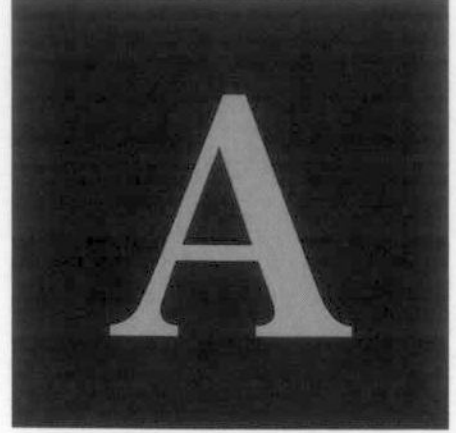

ll I'm saying is that Keth's been spending a *lot* of time with his new Jedi friend. *Too* much time if you ask me."

"I didn't," said Piralli. The Sullustan was perched on his regular stool at the bar, head bowed over his drink in the low light. From the other side of the bar, Kradon—the insectile impresario of Enlightenment—issued an odd, trilling chuckle.

Moona fixed Piralli with a confused look. "You didn't what?"

"Ask you," said Piralli, looking up with a grin. "I didn't ask you."

"Ask me *what*?"

Piralli rolled his eyes. "Never mind. Besides, Keth's *working*. You know that. It's all to do with that peace treaty, between Eiram and E'ronoh. Things haven't been going so well. Someone tried to sabotage the signing with a bomb. The Jedi are doing their best to hold everything together and stop the two worlds sliding back into war. Keth's helping. He and that Jedi are right in the thick of things."

"Hmmm," said Moona, she took a long draw of blue mappa, then wiped her mouth with the back of her hand. "Well, you know how I feel about *Jedi*."

"I think we *all* do," said Piralli.

"It's the arrogance of them," said Moona, wagging a finger. "The way they just assume they know best. That they're the *only* ones who can protect the galaxy."

Piralli shrugged. "They do a pretty good job from where I'm sitting."

"You would say that."

"Why would I?"

"Because you love all those stories, don't you? All that action and adventure on the frontier."

"Well, it's gotta beat working at the docks on Jedha, doesn't it?"

"Careful what you wish for, Piralli. That's what I always tell Keth. Adventure has a way of biting people on the backside. Me? I much prefer the quiet life."

"Something tells me Keth and his new friend wouldn't agree," said Piralli.

"Well, he can't say I didn't warn him," replied Moona. She eyed the door. "Anyway, he's not the only one with a new friend."

Piralli was intrigued. "He's not?"

"Nope," said Moona. "And I'm going to introduce you to her tonight. So, you'd better be on your best behavior."

Piralli laughed. "Who is she, then, this friend? And where did you meet her? You never leave this place."

"You'll see. And I *do* have a life outside of this place. You're just not paying attention." Moona placed her empty glass on the bar and glanced around again at the sound of someone coming through the door. For a moment she looked disappointed, and then narrowed her gaze before turning to Piralli. "I've never seen that uniform before."

Piralli craned his neck. The newcomer looked human, with dark skin and braided hair, and was wearing a neat blue tunic trimmed with gold. He approached the bar and leaned heavily upon it with his forearms, giving his order to the Ithorian barkeep. He looked exhausted. "An Eirami security officer, by the look of him," said Piralli, his voice low. "We've seen a few of them down at the docks, escorting the ambassador to the peace conference."

"From one of the warring planets?" said Moona, studying the newcomer with interest. He caught her looking and gave a little wave. She glanced at Piralli, uncertain, as the man collected his drink from old Chantho and moved along the bar to join them.

Piralli turned in his seat. "You look like you've earned that," he said, nodding at the tall glass of ale the man was holding.

The newcomer's lips twitched. "You could say that." He raised his glass in salute and then downed half its content in a single, long draw.

"Moona. Piralli," said Moona.

"Paternok," replied the man. He placed his drink on the counter. "It's nice to finally find a place worth visiting on this dust bowl."

Piralli laughed. "You're missing the ocean, I take it?"

Paternok looked at Piralli, surprised. "You know Eiram?"

Piralli shook his head. "Only what I've heard from the ground crew of your shuttles." He plucked at his own uniform by way of explanation. "I work at the docks."

"Well, you're missing out. It's more beautiful than you could ever imagine. Crystal-clear oceans stretching as far as the eye can see. The light—it creates this haze in the morning that fills the sky—and you can stand on the shore and believe there's

The blaster clattered noisily to the floor. Silence rippled through the bar.

nothing else in the whole of the galaxy but you and those dancing colors. There's no place quite like it."

"It sounds wet," said Moona. "And salty. I prefer the desert sands."

The man laughed. "I suppose everyone has a different idea of home."

"Sounds like it's been a while," said Piralli, "since you were back there, I mean."

Paternok nodded. "*Too* long. This war… it's changed everything. Ambassador Cerox—that's who I'm assigned to protect—she's spent much of the last five years flitting from world to world across the frontier, trying to drum up support for the war effort. Even when I do get home, it's not the same. Not anymore. Everything seems… Well, it's hard to admire the beauty of a place while bombs are dropping all around you."

"I can't begin to imagine," said Piralli.

"Still, it serves to remind me what we're fighting for," said Paternok. "For home. For the life we had before the war."

"I thought the war was over?" said Piralli. "That's why you're here, isn't it?"

Paternok shrugged. "If the stories are to be believed. The heirs of Eiram and E'ronoh have married and are intent on forging this treaty to end the war. But it's not as simple as just signing a piece of paper and taking some marriage vows, is it?"

"It's not?"

"No." Paternok's expression darkened. He took another long drink of ale. "Thing is, there're people on both sides of this conflict who have lost loved ones. Friends. *Family.* We've spent five years fighting E'ronoh. Even longer hating them. And now we're expected to put all that aside and pretend we're friends, just because of a royal wedding and the word of a few people on Jedha?"

Moona shifted on her stool. She was continually glancing in the direction of the door, but her new friend—whoever she was—had yet to appear. "But surely you *want* to see an end to the fighting, don't you?"

Paternok nodded. "Of course. But it doesn't mean we can forgive. Or forget."

"How did it all start?" asked Moona.

Piralli followed her gaze as she glanced up at another newcomer who'd come through the door. A tall, pale woman with auburn hair that she wore scraped back in a tight bun. She was dressed in a green jacket brocaded with the finery of some official office or position. The left sleeve was pinned across her chest, suggesting she was missing an arm.

The woman exchanged a few words with the looming Gloovan bouncers, the Twinkle Sisters, and then made a beeline for the bar. Piralli bristled. He knew that uniform by sight, too—the newcomer was some sort of representative from E'ronoh—the other party in the war that Paternok had, until recently, been fighting. He turned back to Paternok, who was still talking to Moona.

"…when E'ronoh began to rain bombs down on Eiram without provocation."

Piralli glanced at the woman standing at the bar. He saw her shoulders droop with an embattled sigh. "That's not exactly how it happened, is it?" she said, wearily.

Paternok looked up, his eyes widening at the sight of the uniformed woman. His hand went straight for the concealed holster under his left arm—and the blaster that was hidden inside it. "Damn E'ronhi!" His face was contorted in a look that was somewhere between fear, alarm, and abject hatred.

The blaster came up and out—and was promptly knocked from Paternok's hand by a swift downward chop from Kradon, who had, surreptitiously, managed to slide out from behind the bar to intercept the drawing of the weapon.

The blaster clattered noisily to the floor. Silence rippled through the bar. All eyes settled on the three figures—Paternok, Kradon, and the newcomer.

The woman shrugged, sat down at the bar, and looked expectantly at old Chantho. "I've heard this is the only place to get a decent retsa on the whole of Jedha."

Chantho made a low nodding gesture and reached for the bottle from behind the bar.

Piralli realized he was holding his breath and let it out. Moona was sitting ▸

on the very edge of her stool, watching Kradon, her empty drink in her hand.

The Villerandi made a clacking sound with his mandibles. "*Everyone* is welcome in Enlightenment," he said to Paternok.

The Eirami glanced at his blaster on the floor. He looked torn. Here, before him, was a woman who represented everything he'd been fighting against for the last five years. The cause of every dead soldier he'd known. Here was the *enemy* standing there, blatantly ordering a drink. No matter that their leaders were about to sign an accord—that didn't change how these people on the ground might feel. Piralli thought he could understand that. But then, these two were here as part of the *peace* delegation. No matter what Paternok had said about lack of trust, about his inability to forgive—he wasn't going to be given a choice *but* to find common ground with those he had come to think of as the enemy.

"But how can you let *her*…" said Paternok, obviously torn.

"*Everyone*," repeated Kradon. "*All* beings are welcome… so long as they abstain from violence, and do not engage in theological debate." Kradon seemed to shudder at the very thought.

The moment stretched. And then, clearly deciding that going against Kradon was an inadvisable course of action, Paternok simply sighed. His head drooped.

Kradon clapped a hand on the man's shoulder, pushing him gently, but firmly, back onto his stool. "Now, Kradon sees you have made some new friends. And your glasses are empty! Why don't you all relax and have another drink, hmmm? Kradon believes it was Piralli's round."

Before Piralli could object, Kradon had slipped back behind the bar and begun preparing another three drinks.

Piralli sighed. He supposed it *had* been his round. Nothing went unnoticed in this place. *Especially* by Kradon. A quick glance at the floor told him the dropped blaster had been spirited away by the Villerandi's nimble fingers, too.

The E'ronhi woman accepted her drink from old Chantho. She eyed them cautiously over the rim of her glass. "Kimbral," she said. "In case you were wondering."

Moona affected the usual brief introductions. When it came to Paternok, she hesitated, glanced at him as if seeking permission, and when met with a blank expression introduced him regardless. Kimbral sipped her drink in silent acknowledgement.

"So, you fought in the war too? Is that how you lost your arm?" asked Moona. Piralli rolled his eyes. Moona was ever the tactful one.

Kimbral's lips twitched in the ghost of a smile, but the warmth never reached her eyes. "The Battle of Salamento Bridge," she said. "Worst thing I've ever seen. I was a pilot. An experienced one at that. But flying through that storm of surface-to-air fire… I lost seventeen friends that day. *Seventeen.* Their ships erupting like tiny suns on the horizon. And I was one of the *lucky* ones. When I got hit, it only cost me a limb." She drained half the contents of her glass. "I swear to you—you can't imagine anything quite so hellish as that place."

"I can." All heads turned to regard Paternok, who was gripping his drink so tightly that his knuckles had turned white.

"You were there?" asked Kimbral.

"I still remember the smell of searing ozone when the laser batteries discharged. The scream of rending metal. The afterglow of the explosions lighting up the whole sky." He looked away. "You weren't the only one who lost people that day. My brother. My wife…" He sniffed, then cleared his throat, unable or unwilling to continue.

There was a moment's silence, in which the only sound was the noise of the unusually boisterous crowds coming from somewhere outside.

"I'm sorry," said Kimbral.

Paternok turned, his eyes accusing. "For *what*? For being part of the bombing raid? For starting the war in the first place?"

"For everything we've both lost. For *everyone*. For all that the war has cost us." She chewed her lip. "It doesn't really matter who started things, does it? We both think

"I still remember the smell of searing ozone when the laser batteries discharged."

the other side is to blame. But really, what matters is that we find a way to make it *stop*. Before either of us loses anyone else."

Paternok swallowed. He seemed to consider her words for a moment. "Perhaps you're right." He ran a hand through his hair. "I just... I just want it all to end. We might not be able to forgive or forget, but perhaps we don't have to. Perhaps it is enough to just *stop*."

"I'll drink to that," said Kimbral, raising her glass.

Paternok studied her for a moment, and then nodded and raised his own glass in salute.

"There, now," said Moona. "That wasn't so bad, was it? This peacekeeping business is easy. Who needs the Jedi?"

The two veterans turned their gazes on Moona, and both erupted into racking fits of laughter. But Moona was studying the closed door again.

"I'm sure your friend will be here soon," said Piralli, sensing Moona's agitation.

"It's not that," said Moona. "Can't you hear?"

"The crowds?"

"No." She waved the others quiet.

Piralli strained to listen. "That noise... It sounds like *blaster* fire!"

Kradon was already making for the door. He pushed his way between the Twinkle Sisters to peer out at the scene beyond. "Kradon does not like the look of this," he muttered.

Piralli, Moona and the others hurried over.

Outside, people were scattering for cover as ships slid noisily overhead, deploying scores of enforcer droids, strange-looking weapons platforms, and platoons of uniformed soldiers to the nearby streets. Streaks of blaster fire raked the tops of distant buildings. Somewhere close by, people were screaming.

"Those are Eirami soldiers!" said Paternok, his voice tight. "Cerox must have deployed the troops."

"And those are E'ronhi ships, too," added Kimbral.

"Then the peace talks have failed," said Kradon. "And now your war has come to Jedha."

For a moment, none of them spoke as the gravity of those words gradually sank in.

Slowly, Kimbral turned to Paternok, her expression wracked with sorrow. "I... I..." she faltered, and then drew herself up as she collected herself. "It was good to know you, Eirami."

Paternok nodded. "Likewise, E'ronhi."

Without another word, Kimbral pushed her way out past the Twinkle Sisters and out of Enlightenment. Before long she had disappeared, swallowed beneath the shadow of a passing ship.

"No," said Moona, quietly, as if her simple denial could prevent the horror unfolding before their eyes. As if it could stop Kimbral from returning to the fight.

Paternok dusted the front of his uniform and took a step forward, but Piralli caught his arm, holding him back. "You're not going out there, are you? To fight?"

Paternok gently shook him off. "What choice do I have?"

"Just now, in there," Piralli indicated the bar behind him, "you were ready to give it up, to draw a truce. You said you just wanted it all to stop."

"Looks like that's been taken out of our hands," said Paternok. "But all the same, I thank you, my friends, for the chance to dream of peace. Even if it was only for a moment."

He ducked out through the door, running for the cover of a nearby side street. Another ship screeched low over the nearby rooftops, discharging its blasters.

Piralli turned back to the bar, shaking his head. "Well, whatever's going on out there, I want no part in it. I suggest we take cover in here, sit out th—"

"Incoming," barked Delphine, cutting him off.

"What do you mean, 'incoming'?" said Piralli, turning just in time to see a tall human male, shouting obscenities, and wielding a metal bar as a makeshift cudgel, run directly into the towering Gloovan's fist. The man went down with a thud. But others were following in his wake. Rioters, by the look of them, and they appeared to be *exceedingly* angry.

Somewhere in the distance, a building exploded.

"Back up, back up!" bellowed Kradon, his voice acquiring a sharp, shrill pitch that Piralli had never heard him use before. "It looks like Kradon has some very thirsty customers to deal with."

But no one was laughing. Not this time.

As Piralli fell back, grabbing for Moona's hand, the swarm of rioters closed on Enlightenment's doors.

TO BE CONTINUED

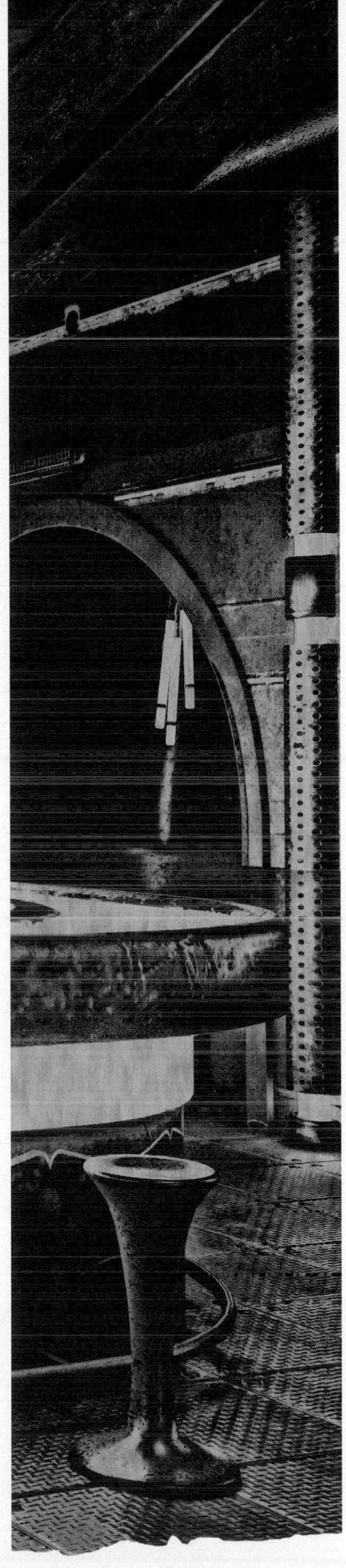

TALES OF ENLIGHTENMENT

"No Such Thing as a Bad Customer"

PART TWO

By George Mann

Concept art by Andrée Wallin

Previously, in a galaxy far, far away....

Violence has erupted on the streets of Jedha, and the regulars of the Enlightenment cantina find themselves hemmed in by frenzied rioters and and a phalanx of enforcer droids.

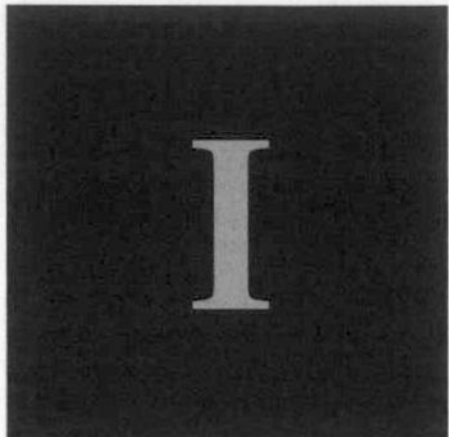

It had started badly, and it was getting worse by the minute. Piralli buried his head in the crook of his arms to protect himself from another shower of broken glass, as a stray shot from an enforcer droid detonated several bottles of Kradon's finest liquor on the bar above his head. He could hear Enlightenment's famed impresario bellowing angrily as he returned fire with a blaster rifle several meters away.

Flicking shards of broken bottle from his shoulders, Piralli glanced at Moona, who was similarly taking shelter behind the bar, along with the Ithorian barkeep, Old Chantho, and the Iktotchi electro-harpist, Madelina, who looked terrified. This was only natural, given the circumstances—they were in the middle of a full-on invasion, after all.

Moona met Piralli's gaze and shook her head in apparent bewilderment, setting her head tails dancing. It seemed she couldn't quite fathom what was going on, either.

It had all happened so fast. One moment they'd been standing in the doorway, about to be charged by a stampede of angry rioters, the next Kradon had flung them back here for shelter while the bar came under siege. And now a small Twi'lek Jedi—*a Jedi!*—was performing backflips overhead, whipping her blue lightsaber back and forth as she deflected lancing bolts of blaster fire.

Piralli had almost given up trying to piece it all together. He knew that Camille and Delphine had dealt with the first wave of rioters easily enough, but before they had a chance to even catch their breaths, a whole contingent of refugees had arrived, pouring into the bar at the behest of two Jedi (the Twi'lek and a bearded human), who'd rescued them from a collapsing building elsewhere in the city. Apparently, the whole of Jedha was gripped in a riotous frenzy, a *battle*, and Enlightenment was deemed the safest place to be.

Well, look how well that's turning out.

One of the Jedi, the human male named Vildar *something-or-other*, had made a run for it through the smuggler's tunnel beneath Enlightenment—something to do with a rescue mission. The other, the young Twi'lek female named Matty, had stayed behind to help defend the bar and look after the refugees—who, it turned out, were mostly members of the Path of the Open Hand, the strange sect and protest group who were supposed to *hate* all Jedi. Piralli hadn't quite figured that one out, yet, but he supposed the Jedi were famed for helping *everyone*, after all, no matter their creed or beliefs.

There'd been an attempt to flee through the tunnels in the wake of the human Jedi, to get out into the desert and away from the city, but then the tunnels had collapsed due to the percussive shockwaves of bombardments from above, and now everyone who remained in the tapbar was trapped.

That wouldn't have been so bad, if it hadn't been for the army of enforcer droids that had breached the rear

The whole of Jedha was gripped in a riotous frenzy, a battle, and Enlightenment was deemed the safest place to be.

"What the hell is going on?" Pirالli bellowed to Moona, cringing as more errant blaster shots scorched the bar.

entrance and were pressing the attack, or the angry mob of rioters who were still trying to break through the main doors on the other side.

What made matters *worse* was the fact the only thing stopping them all from being killed was the young Jedi, probably just a *Padawan*, and a wounded Sorcerer of Tund who claimed to be part of the city's new Force council, the so-called 'Convocation.' Oh, and Kradon, who was blasting away at the droids with gleeful abandon.

"What the hell is going on?" Piralli bellowed to Moona, cringing as more errant blaster shots scorched the bar above their heads. Moona scooted closer, keeping her head down.

"It's the Jedi," she said, flatly.

"I *know* about the Jedi," said Piralli, fighting exasperation. "But why are those droids attacking us? And what do the rioters *want*?"

Moona rolled her eyes. "That's what I mean," she said, jabbing her finger as the Jedi in question, Matty, slid along the bar, her lightsaber razing the wooden surface as she fought to steady herself. She glanced down at Piralli and shot him a wink, before leaping off again in a flurry of precisely timed movements that saw at least six blaster shots redirected away from the gaggle of refugees, who were huddled behind a loose barricade of tables at the far end of the main bar. "The droids want the Jedi. She's the one who's brought all this down on us, don't you see?"

"But she came here looking for shelter for the wounded," said Piralli.

Moona shrugged. "That may well be the case, but think about it, Piralli. It's just made everything worse for the rest of us. The rioters outside want to get to the Path of the Open Hand, because they think those refugees are responsible for whatever is going on out there, and the droids want to get at the Jedi, because they probably are the ones responsible."

"How can they be?" said Piralli. "You know it was the Eiram and E'ronoh troops who deployed their forces and started the battle. That's got nothing to do with the Jedi. As far as I can see, this one's trying to help."

"It has *everything* to do with the Jedi. They were supposed to be overseeing the peace conference. They brought Eiram and E'ronoh here, to Jedha, in the first place. Remember, that's what Keth's been doing. Mixing with all those Jedi and highfalutin officials."

Piralli's head was thumping. He flinched at the sound of more explosions close by. Thoughts of their friend being stuck out there amongst the worst of the fighting made his stomach flip. "What if Keth's out there, somewhere? What if he's hurt?"

Moona chewed her lip. "I've been thinking the same thing. And Erta, too."

"Erta?"

"My *friend*, remember? She was coming here to meet me. So I could introduce you." Piralli could see the genuine concern in Moona's expression. Everything was such a mess.

"I'm sure she'll be okay," he said, but he could hear the quavering in his own voice. "I'm sure they both will."

Moona nodded emphatically, clearly willing it to be true. "Yeah. Yeah, they will." She ducked low as a bar stool clattered into the rack of bottles above their heads, showering them in spilled liquor. "Not so sure we can say the same about us though," she said, attempting a smile. It didn't reach her eyes.

Piralli dabbed something blue and sticky from his face. From across the room, the sound of a child whimpering tugged at his heart. "Maybe not, but I'm damned if I'm going to cower here for much longer. There are people who need help." He turned and started shuffling across the floor on his hands and knees.

"Wait! Where are you *going*?" He ▸

There were at least a dozen of the enforcer droids clamoring around a ragged hole in the wall.

heard Moona setting out after him and paused, turning back.

"I'm going to do what I can to help those people." He gestured in the direction of the refugees.

"But what can you do?" implored Moona. "You're going to get yourself killed!"

"I don't know, Moona. I have no idea. But I have to do *something*. I can't sit around behind the bar, hoping that a lone Jedi and a wounded sorcerer are going to save us all. I have to *try*. If I'm going to die in this mess, then at least I'll die *doing* something."

Moona nodded. She looked back, patted Old Chantho on the arm and gave Madelina a little wave, and then hurried after him, crunching through the fragments of broken glass on the ground. "Okay, you win. What's the plan?"

"I don't *have* a plan!"

Moona sighed. "Then why don't we start with the wounded? Focus on helping anyone in immediate danger"

"Good idea." Piralli decided it probably wouldn't be politic to point out they were *all* in immediate danger. More danger than he'd ever been in before. The thought filled him with dread, but he pushed it down, trying to focus.

Keep busy, Piralli. Make a difference.

He scurried along to the edge of the bar, peeking around to try to get a sense of what was happening. His eyes widened at the sight. There were at least a dozen of the enforcer droids clamoring around a ragged hole in the wall, where they'd blasted their way through to the interior of the bar. Their sinister red eyes swiveled constantly, focusing on their next targets. Matty, the Twi'lek Jedi, was still frantically battering away a storm of blaster shots, but the exertion was clearly taking its toll, and her expression was severe and weary. Beside her, the Sorcerer of Tund—Piralli hadn't managed to catch his name in the chaos—stood with his feet planted, his arms held wide, and strain evident on his face, as if he was holding back some invisible, physical barrier against which the enforcer droids were throwing themselves, attempting to break through.

"They won't be able to keep it up," said Moona, from over his shoulder. "No one could."

"They have to," muttered Piralli. "There's nothing else between us and those murderous droids."

"I know." Moona's voice seemed to catch in her throat. "Come on." She launched herself into the open, keeping her head down as she ran, throwing herself down behind the makeshift barrier that was all that separated the refugees from the raging battle.

Piralli swallowed, and then followed suit.

The refugees looked even more terrified than he'd imagined. Most were dressed in the simple cloth robes favored by the Path of the Open Hand. Many of them were carrying minor injuries but were being treated as best as possible by others of the Path, who were binding cuts, fixing slings, and applying salves to blaster burns. At least two of the injured had died in situ, and people were hunched over their still bodies, weeping and muttering prayers.

Close to Piralli, a stray blaster shot seared a hole in the wall. He glanced round. The overturned tables were hardly any sort of barrier at all, not in the face of the sort of weapons being deployed by the droids. But there wasn't enough room to get everyone behind the bar, either.

They were stuck, reliant on the Jedi and the sorcerer to keep the droids at bay. The only way out of this mess was to find some way to help them.

"Moona? Moona!" Piralli turned at the sound of someone calling Moona's name. A small human woman with brown skin and wide eyes was pushing her way through the press of refugees, coming their way.

"*Erta*!" The relief on Moona's face was telling. Tears brimmed in her eyes. She darted forward, wrapping Erta into a long, heartfelt embrace. They kissed, long and deep, and then Moona prized herself free, holding Erta by the shoulders and looking her up and down. "I thought…" She steadied her breathing. "You're okay? You're not hurt? I was worried—"

Erta grinned. "I'm okay. Well, not hurt, at least. I was there when the almshouse came down. I tried to help. I stuck with the Jedi as they seemed to know what they were doing."

Moona rolled her eyes, but the relief was evident. She looked at Erta with such fondness, such *love*, that Piralli felt a catch in his own throat. Moona really did have a life outside the bar. A happy one. And to think—today she'd been finally planning to introduce Piralli to her girlfriend.

"I'm Piralli," he said awkwardly.

Erta grinned. "Yeah, I've heard a *lot* about you."

Piralli was about to crack a joke about meeting in better circumstances, when more blaster fire raked the wall close to his head; he turned, appalled, to see one of the enforcer droids had breached the Jedi's defenses and was swooping in their direction, its blaster spitting burning rounds.

He shoved Moona and Erta backwards, sending them both sprawling, turning to face the droid as it closed, only meters away. Its bland, impassive face was the last thing he was ever going to see. But at least he'd helped his friend. At least—

The droid stuttered, issued an odd, strangled beep, and then crumpled to the floor, bisected by the searing plasma of Matty's lightsaber. She nodded at Piralli, then glanced down at Moona and Erta, who were scrambling to pick themselves up off the floor.

Matty grinned. "Another Twi'lek! Nice to meet you. I'm Matty!" She pivoted, whipping her lightsaber back and forth to deflect more shots from the droids, who were still clamoring to force their way through the opening they'd blasted in the wall. Matty glanced back at Moona. "Talk later!" And then she was off again, flipping balletically as she spun her lightsaber in a protective wheel.

Moona met Piralli's gaze. "Damned Jedi," she said. And then erupted into a fit of nervous laughter.

"It's no use laughing," hissed a tall, male Dressellian, who was crouched low behind an upturned table. He was wearing robes that suggested he held some sort of official position at the Temple of the Kyber. "We'll probably all be dead in a few minutes. Those Jedi were supposed to protect us!"

"Oh, shut up," said Moona. "Only I get to criticize the Jedi here."

The Dressellian gave an indignant huff.

"We need a plan," said Piralli. "We have to help them find a way to stop those droids."

"But we don't have any weapons," said Erta. "How are we going to stop that many droids without blasters?"

"Electricity," said Moona. "We overload their circuits. Cause them to burn out."

"I like your thinking," said Piralli. "That could work. But how do we even start?"

"Easy," said Moona.

"Easy?"

"Yeah. We use Madelina's electro-harp. We rig up the speakers by the sides of that hole in the wall, then turn off the safeties and overload the harp. When someone strikes a chord, the speakers will blow and discharge the excess current into anything close by."

Piralli and Erta peered at Moona. "And you know this, how?"

Moona shot Piralli a cocky grin. "I told you. I have a life outside

The droid stuttered, issued an odd, strangled beep, and then crumpled to the floor.

Enlightenment. It's what I do. I drink and I know stuff."

Piralli laughed. "You mean you've fantasized about blowing up that harp before, haven't you?"

"You can't prove that," said Moona, with a shrug. "But yeah. Haven't we all?"

Piralli was just glad Madelina couldn't hear them over the noise of the raging battle. "Okay. Let's do it. We'll crawl around the other side of the bar, and up onto the stage from there. And you can explain it all to your new friend, too," he said, indicating Matty with a nod of his head.

"Whatever," said Moona.

"You're all mad," muttered the Dressellian. "All mad!"

"Are the speakers in place?"

"Almost!" Piralli huffed as he and Erta dragged the last of the tall speaker units into position. They'd set them up on either side of the ragged breach in the wall, where the droids were still fighting to get through.

Piralli was impressed. Whatever her feelings about the Jedi Order, Moona had been good to her word. She'd explained the plan briefly to Matty—who'd seemed honestly relieved to have some support and backup—before retreating to the stage area, where she'd set to work stripping out the safety protocols on the electro-harp.

Meanwhile, things in the rest of the bar were getting worse. Kradon had temporarily stopped unloading blaster shots into the wall of enforcer droids to focus on strengthening the barricade holding the bar's front doors in place. The noise of the angry rioters was growing with every passing minute, and it sounded as though they'd soon be forcing their way inside too.

Not only that, but an increasing amount of blaster shots were slipping past Matty's tiring defenses. One had already struck a civilian in the arm, and that infuriating Dressellian seemed intent on stirring up dissent amongst the walking wounded. The Sorcerer of Tund looked exhausted, too, and Piralli noticed he was bleeding from a wound in his midriff, his robes stained dark and wet. They were running out of time. They had to make this work.

"All right. We're ready," he called.

On the stage, Moona was sitting before the electro-harp. "Whenever you're ready, then," she said in reply.

Matty shot Piralli a glance. "You're *certain* this is going to work?"

Piralli swallowed. He looked at Moona, then Erta, then back at Matty. "Yes. I trust Moona."

"Good enough for me," said Matty. She waved him and Erta back, taking a few tentative steps herself, her lightsaber still thrumming. "Tarna?"

The Sorcerer of Tund, sagging now with the strain, met her eye and nodded. He lowered his arms.

The enforcer droids swarmed through the breach. Piralli counted six, seven, eight of them, before they were just a jumble of silver limbs and blasters.

Matty frowned as the droids pushed closer, until they were almost on top of them, positioned squarely between the two huge speakers. "Moona...?"

"Cover your ears."

Moona struck the strings of the harp.

For a moment, nothing happened. Then the sound struck like a thunderclap, so loud that Piralli's eardrums felt as if they were bursting. Light flashed, bright as the noonday sun, and tendrils of crackling electricity shot out from the ruptured speakers, striking the metallic droids, and scuttling over their outer shells, frying circuits and causing photoreceptors to detonate in their sockets.

The enforcer droids swarmed through the breach. Piralli counted six, seven, eight of them.

Behind them, the front doors finally caved under the force of the rioters' sustained blows.

It was over in seconds. By the time Piralli regained some control of his senses, the droids had been reduced to nothing but a heap of spitting, jerking shells, wreathed in a pall of black smoke. Erta was furiously kissing Moona on the stage, while the wounded members of the Path of the Open Hand were walking about in dazed shock.

Piralli felt a hand on his shoulder and turned to see Kradon. The Villerandi was looking down at the wreckage of the speakers, his face creased in sorrow. "Kradon had those imported from Coruscant," he lamented. "Hand crafted. No expense spared." He sighed. "But still, maybe your friend Moona can patch them up again, eh?"

Behind them, the front doors finally caved under the force of the rioters' sustained blows. They swung open on broken hinges. The rioters began to spill inside.

Piralli heard Matty's lightsaber reignite.

He watched as the lead rioters took in the scene: dozens of angry faces, surrounded by scores of ruined enforcer droids, and an impatient-looking Jedi brandishing her lightsaber as though she'd really had enough of all this.

The rioters looked from Kradon, to Piralli, to Moona, to the Twinkle Sisters...

...and then slowly backed out again, disappearing into the street.

Piralli felt a flood of relief. He leaned on the bar, his mind whirling. "It's over."

Matty shook her head. "I only wish that were true." She walked wearily to the door; her lightsaber now extinguished. "But I fear it's only just beginning."

All around the bar, people were picking themselves up from the ground, helping one another. Madelina was looking forlornly at the sparking ruins of her harp. Old Chantho was pouring people shots of whatever stiff drinks still sat in full bottles behind the bar. Even the sour-faced archivist who'd spent the entire time moaning was doing his bit, helping to disassemble the barricade to free the trapped refugees from the Path of the Open Hand. Moon and Erta were in each other's arms. Kradon was tending to Tarna's grevious wounds.

Enlightenment was pulling together. Just like it always did. Everything was going to be okay.

Piralli took a glass of retsa from Old Chantho and, with a brief nod of appreciation, knocked it back in one gulp. His palate stung, but it felt good.

He pushed himself up from the bar. The Jedi, Matty, was still standing alone in the street, just outside the open door. He wandered over to join her, ducking out into the bright afternoon light.

The sight that greeted him rocked him to his core.

The city square was in ruins. War machines lay toppled on their sides, while ships flitted overhead, unleashing a storm of fire on the buildings below. Matty had been right. The battle was far from over. And it was far worse than he could have possibly imagined.

He could see corpses laying in the street where they'd fallen, abandoned by their loved ones as they'd hurried for cover.

"No... I..." he didn't have the words.

Matty let out a long exhalation. "I know."

Everywhere, the city was burning. And all Piralli could think about was those who had lost their lives in the crossfire.

Jedha was supposed to be a place of faith. Of sanctity. Of *peace.*

Today, it had become a place of wanton violence, of death.

Overwhelmed, he fell to his knees, and wept.

THE END

TALES OF ENLIGHTENMENT

"Last Orders"

By George Mann

Concept art by Will Htay and Vincent Jenkins

Previously, in a galaxy far, far away....

Life on Jedha is beginning to return to normal following the violent upheaval that rocked the world. But for the regulars of the Enlightenment cantina, the events have left a tragic mark.

Piralli sipped his drink. The day was growing long, and Enlightenment was starting to fill up with its usual assortment of locals, pilgrims, hapless passers-through and rogues out to make a credit or two at the expense of the rest. In fact, the place was as busy as he'd ever seen it.

Old Chantho was rushed off his feet behind the bar, helped—and Piralli used the word loosely—by the ever-gregarious Kradon, who at that moment was entertaining a group of four female Togrutas with talk of his days as the master of a traveling dance troupe. Piralli knew the story was as manufactured as Kradon's outlandish cheer, but it made him smile all the same. He watched as the Villerandi filled their glasses again and slid their credits under the bar.

Madelina had, sadly, managed to obtain a replacement electroharp, and was busy plucking at the strings, head tossed back, lost in the same shrill wail that had plagued Piralli's existence for the last few years. He supposed he'd grown to like it, really. Not that he'd ever admit as much. Especially to Moona.

The Twinkle Sisters stood at their posts on either side of the door, arms folded, sullen expressions writ large on their rotund faces.

It had only been a few months since the end of the horrific battle that had temporarily seized Jedha in its grip, but things were already beginning to return to normal.

The warring planets of Eiram and E'ronoh had made some early reparations, and the Guardians of the Whills had helped oversee the restoration of order throughout the city. The twin chancellors of the Republic had shipped in platoons of peacekeeping soldiers to assist the locals with the clearing and reconstruction work.

Aside from the Protector, the ancient statue of the Jedi that had fallen outside the city walls, most of the important monuments and ancient buildings had survived, if not unscathed, then at least in a repairable state.

Take Enlightenment, which had suffered so much damage during the siege by the enforcer droids that Piralli had worried that it could never be restored to its former glory. Or perhaps at all.

He'd been wrong though, proving that ingenuity, camaraderie, hard work and Kradon's somewhat questionable connections really could achieve anything.

The rear wall had been rebuilt, the bar restocked, the doors reinforced, and the stools righted. Even the scorch marks caused by the explosion and the pock marks in the walls left by the blaster shots had somehow just been... swept away. Like so much broken glass.

Enlightenment went on, as it always had.

Not everything was the same, though. Not all losses could be so easily accounted for, patched over, or made better with plaster and brushes and a fresh coat of paint.

Some bit much deeper.

To Piralli's left, a single stool stood empty at the bar. No one had sat on it since the tapbar had reopened. No one wanted to forget. Piralli supposed it was a form of respect, an honoring of the lost. And maybe just a dash of wishful thinking, hoping that, by keeping the seat free, somehow, they might conjure their dead friend back to life.

The stool had been the favored seat of Keth Cerapath, the acolyte from the

Enlightenment went on, as it always had. Not everything was the same, though.

Keth had died in the way he had always lived —helping others.

Church of the Force who had been a regular at Enlightenment. Piralli's friend. One of the best people he'd ever known.

Keth had died in the way he had always lived—helping others. He'd found the adventure he'd always craved, at the side of the Jedi Knight Silandra Sho, and had not only assisted her in her mission to discover the truth behind the bombings that had ignited the battle but had saved hundreds of people by leading them to shelter in the Dome of Deliverance after the fighting had commenced.

Silandra Sho had paid tribute to Keth, visiting the bar just a few weeks earlier to tell his story.

It had helped. Piralli was so proud of his friend. So very proud. He'd finally fulfilled his ambitions. He'd become the person he'd always wanted to be. And for that, Piralli could only be grateful.

The stool, though—that would remain empty. It was only right.

Piralli eyed the door. Still no sign of Moona. Since she'd met Erta, she'd been present a bit less in the bar. Which, he supposed, was a good thing. She was getting on with her life. And yet, Piralli hoped that she didn't forget about him, and Keth, and this place that they'd made their own. They'd all been through too much together for that.

As it transpired, he needn't have worried. A few moments later she came bustling in, her arm draped around Erta's shoulder. Both were smiling brightly.

Conspiratorially.

They hurried over to Piralli. Moona placed a small cloth knapsack on the bar.

"Hey, hey, Piralli. What's new?"

Moona caught Old Chantho's eye, and he waved a brief hand in acknowledgement. Moments later, two drinks were on the bar beside Moona's knapsack, despite the press of other patrons waiting to be served.

Piralli eyed Moona suspiciously. "Nothing's new," he said. "At least, not with me." He glanced at the knapsack. "You, on the other hand…?"

Moona beamed at him.

"Show him," urged Erta, nudging Moona with her elbow. "It's not fair to keep him waiting."

Moona feigned resignation. "Where's the fun in that?" Despite her words, though, she was clearly anxious to show Piralli the contents of the bag. She was practically hopping from foot to foot in excitement.

"Is everything okay, Moona?" said Piralli.

"Oh, yeah. Everything's good," she said. "Take a look at my new acquisition."

Piralli watched as she removed the object from the knapsack and placed it carefully on the bar. She stood back, regarding it proudly.

It was a small, black box, made from some kind of stone or polished glass.

"Well?" She looked at Piralli expectantly.

"Well, *what*?"

"What do you think?"

"I think…" He frowned, peering at the unusual object. "I think it looks like an old box."

Moona rolled her eyes.

Erta grinned. "It is. But not just *any* old box. She got it from Spinran, down at the docks."

Piralli nearly spat out his drink. "Spinran! What are doing, Moona? You should know he can't be trusted."

Spinran, a Halisite with a huge bone crest on his head that flushed red and blue depending on his mood, was a dock worker, like Piralli. But unlike Piralli, he maintained a little business on the side, selling items of dubious provenance to people who really should know better than to buy such things off a guy whose job it was to scrape clean the hulls of visiting ships.

"Maybe this time he's onto something," said Moona. She patted the box. "This is something special. It has power."

"Power?" Piralli squinted at the ugly thing.

"Yeah," said Erta. "Spinran said it's a Jedi artifact. Claims he found it in the ruins of the Protector, after the dust had cleared."

Piralli twisted in his seat to see a tall, broad-shouldered human male standing behind him.

"But what does it actually *do?*" asked Piralli.

Moona shrugged. "We're not sure yet."

"Keth will—" Piralli turned to glance at the empty stool to his left, his voice catching in his throat. "Keth would have known what it was."

There was a moment of silence.

"Anyway, it's not so long ago you hated Jedi. And now you're their biggest fan?" said Piralli.

"Hardly," said Moona. "But I've been rethinking things, since we've met a few that were all right…"

"You *have* changed your tune," laughed Piralli.

"That Twi'lek, Matty, did save my life," said Erta.

"Exactly," said Moona, emphatically. "And that makes her all right in my book."

"So now you're procuring Jedi artifacts from dodgy backstreet dealers," said Piralli.

Moona turned the box over in her hands. Her eyes seemed to glitter. "I wonder what's in it."

"You mean you haven't opened it?"

"She can't," said Erta. "She's tried everything. But it's sealed shut."

"Just as well," said a voice from over Piralli's shoulder. "Your friend is right. That box is filled with great power. But not the sort you want to go messing around with."

Piralli twisted in his seat to see a tall, broad-shouldered human male standing behind him. He was dressed in Jedi robes, and had his arms folded across his chest.

Not another one…

"And *you* are?" said Piralli.

The Jedi smiled. "Harro. Lee Harro."

The name seemed familiar, but Piralli was sure he would have remembered if they'd met before.

"Hang on. Lee Harro?" said Moona, pushing her way between them. She looked the Jedi up and down, appraising him. "Taller than I imagined."

Harro looked perplexed, but unfazed. "You've heard of me?"

Moona nodded, then punched Piralli lightly on the arm. "Lee Harro! He's the one that prospector told us about. Saretha. The one who got eaten by the plants."

Harro laughed. "Ah. Now things are starting to make sense."

Piralli gawped at the Jedi. "That's *you?*" He took a sip of his drink. "What are you doing *here*? Are you looking for Saretha? If so, you should know that she's already sold that hunk of kyber. She left weeks ago."

Harro smiled. "I'm glad to hear it. Hopefully it helped pay for the repairs to her ship. No. I'm here to help. After the battle…"

"Ah," said Piralli. That *did* make sense.

Harro gestured to the empty stool beside Piralli. "May I?"

Piralli squirmed awkwardly. "Umm, not that one. Sorry."

"It's taken?" said Harro.

"In a manner of speaking."

"It belonged to our friend," said Moona. "He died during the battle."

"I see. I'm sorry," said Harro. "And he would have objected to me sitting here?"

Moona glanced at Piralli. Then shook her head. "Are you kidding! He would have been off that stool like a shot to offer it up to a visiting *Jedi*. Can you imagine?"

Piralli grinned at the thought of Keth's bright face as he hurriedly vacated his seat. "I guess you're right."

"Then…?" said Harro.

Piralli used the edge of his boot to drag out the stool. "We'll make an exception. Just this once."

Harro smiled. He sat down, resting one arm on the bar. Moona and Erta crowded round.

"So, you reckon you know what's in the box?" said Erta.

The Jedi made a noncommittal gesture. "If you have time, I could tell you a short tale that might shed some light."

"We're not going anywhere," said Piralli. "Are we?"

"Nope," said Moona.

"Very well," said Harro. "But I'm going to need a drink."

Moona rolled her eyes again. "Always needy, these Jedi." She slid her own, untouched drink across the bar.

"Much obliged," said Harro. He took a sip of the blue mappa, made an appreciative noise, and then set it down. "My tale begins many millennia ago, when the Old Republic was a very different place, and much of the galaxy remained unexplored. The Jedi Order was strong but opposed by Force users of a different kind, those who chose to wield the power of the dark side, to allow themselves to be ruled by fear and anger."

"The Sith," said Erta, almost reverentially.

Harro nodded. "The Sith. And there was one particular Sith Lord who persecuted the Jedi like no other. His name was Darth Caldoth, and for decades his campaign of terror ran almost unchecked. Many Jedi pitched themselves against him, and most never returned."

Harro took another sip of Moona's drink. "Well, there was one Jedi, a human woman named Pelopy Vus, who decided that her one goal, above all else, was to put an end to Caldoth's reign of terror. She was tired of seeing her fellow Jedi murdered and wanted to save others from the same fate.

"But Vus was wise and knew that if she simply tried to take on Caldoth as the others had, she would surely die too, for Caldoth was a master of the blade, and the power of the dark side leant him a great advantage. She needed a weapon that could put an end to Caldoth once and for all. Something he would never expect."

"A bomb?" said Erta.

Harro laughed, but not unkindly. "No. Something far more arcane. Something that could contain his power. A prison. And so, she began a quest that would last for several years, seeking ancient and arcane knowledge, traveling the breadth of the known galaxy in search of an answer.

"But Caldoth was sly and soon got wind of what Vus was doing. And so, instead of heading her off, he decided to lay a trap, for that was the sort of person he was. He began seeding stories, a carefully laid trail of breadcrumbs that would lead Vus down a dangerous path."

"Like a game?" said Piralli.

"Exactly," said Harro. "Like a Loth-cat toying with its prey. He was careful, only ever giving away enough information for Vus to think she was on the right track, seeding it through the word of agents and unknowing civilians. And, soon enough, Vus had everything she'd been looking for—the necessary instructions for how to build a small, glass box, imbued with the power of ancient rites, that would serve as a kind of prison, drawing the essence out of its victim and sealing them inside its six small walls forever."

Moona stared at him, wide-eyed. "A glass box..."

Harro held up a finger, silencing her while he continued. "But Vus didn't know it was a trap. And, in her haste and desperation to capture Caldoth, she carried out the necessary rituals to create the box, even though the power was derived from the dark side of the Force."

"I don't like where this is leading," said Erta.

"You see, the cleverness of Caldoth's trap is that Vus's plan would have worked, if only she'd properly understood how to use the artifact once it had been created. But Caldoth had been careful to keep that information to himself. And so, when the ritual was finally complete, Vus didn't understand that by opening the box herself..."

"She was trapped in the prison!" said Piralli.

Harro nodded. "The moment she lifted the lid, her essence was drawn out and trapped in the box, leaving just the empty shell of her body behind." He sat back in his stool, eyeing them all with interest.

Moona was now looking at the glass box on the bar in abject horror. "You mean, if I'd opened that thing..."

"My tale begins many millennia ago, when the Old Republic was a very different place."

Moona was now looking at the glass box on the bar in abject horror.

Harro shrugged. "Who knows what might have happened."

Piralli saw Moona swallow. She leaned over and whispered something to Erta, who nodded emphatically. Then, gingerly, Moona picked up the box and tossed it to the Jedi, as if she couldn't get rid of it fast enough. "Here, you have it."

Harro caught it, a quizzical expression on his face. "You want *me* to have it?"

Moona nodded and took a step back. "I don't want anything more to do with it. You can get rid of it, can't you? You're a Jedi. You'll know what to do."

"If you're sure that's what you want…"

Moona held up a hand. "I'm sure. Please, get the thing out of my sight. And I'll be having words with Spinran, too."

"Very well." Harro slipped the box into his robes. He retrieved the glass of blue mappa from the bar and drained it. Then he stood. "Well, it's been nice talking to you all," he said. "But I'd better get this somewhere safe."

"Yes, sure. Thanks," said Moona, who clearly couldn't wait to see the back of him. She gave him a nervous wave and shuffled a bit further along the bar, calling to get Old Chatho's attention.

Harro made for the door, but Piralli hurried after him, catching the Jedi's arm. "That story. Was it real?"

Standing on the threshold, Harro considered his response for a moment. "Well, it was really a story."

"But the events you described—did they actually happen?" pressed Piralli. "Or was it just a legend?"

Harro offered him a sly grin. "Does it matter, so long as there was purpose to the telling and enjoyment in the listening?"

Piralli frowned. "I suppose not."

"All things are possible if you are open to them," said Harro. "Even the outlandish tales of a Jedi."

Piralli glanced back at Moona, who was leaning over the bar, shouting another order to Old Chantho.

He looked back at Harro. "So, what's *really* in the box?"

Harro patted the pocket of his robes and winked. And then he turned and left.

Piralli smiled and shook his head, then returned to his seat, where a fresh drink was already waiting for him.

Moona had her arm around Erta's shoulders again. "Well, that was a close escape," she said, the relief evident on her face. "Thank the Light that Jedi turned up when he did."

Piralli grinned. "Yeah. He knew exactly what he was dealing with."

He looked round. Kradon was tucking Keth's seat neatly back beneath the bar. "Kradon thinks everything is going to be all right," said the Villerandi, and right there and then, surrounded by his friends, Piralli found that he could only agree.

"I think you're right," he said. "It really is."

Kradon clacked his mandibles together. "I'll add the extra credits to your tab, shall I?"

"What credits?" said Piralli.

"Ah, didn't you know? There's a new surcharge. Jedi pay extra."

"But it was *my* drink!" said Moona.

"Kradon understands," said the Villerandi. "But what can I do, hmmm? What can I do? Rules are rules."

Piralli looked at Moona. They both burst into roaring, gut-wrenching laughter. And it felt good.

THE END

TALES OF ENLIGHTENMENT

"Missing Pieces"

By George Mann

Concept art by Matt Allsop

How are the kids, Moona? Been a while since I've seen them." Moona smiled over the rim of her glass. Her eyes sparkled. Piralli loved to see that look on her face, the way she shone whenever she thought of her children. All he'd ever wanted for his friend was happiness, and it gave him a warm glow to know that she'd found it.

They were sitting at the bar in their usual spot, the well-worn stools as comfortable as old gloves.

"Good. Both are back home with Erta, supposedly studying. Though I'm sure they're probably watching some holodrama or other. They have her wrapped around their little fingers."

Piralli laughed. "Not just Erta," he said. "I've seen how you are with them, remember."

Moona shrugged. "They've been through a lot. They deserve to be happy."

"So do you."

She grinned. "I am."

Moona and Erta had adopted the two children—a Klatooinian called Lof and a Weequay called Theeka—after they'd been orphaned during the tumultuous Battle of Jedha, almost five years earlier. They'd been small then, but the last Piralli had seen them, a couple of months previously, they'd been growing up fast, running rings around their indulgent parents. A few years ago, Piralli would never have imagined that Moona would settle down, have kids and become the most responsible out of all of the crew who regularly patronized Enlightenment, but there it was. She was a wonder. And she still made time to keep him company, even if it was only once per week these days.

Moona motioned for Old Chantho to pour them another round of drinks. The Ithorian nodded ponderously and fetched a fresh bottle of blue mappa.

Close by, Kradon was hunched over a table talking to a grizzled old Umbaran with pale blue skin and a bald, scarred head. No doubt some dubious exchange of information was taking place, as per usual.

Moona's life may have dramatically changed, Piralli reflected, but there was a certain comfort to be found in everything at Enlightenment remaining just the same as it always had.

"What about you, then?" said Moona. She brushed droplets of condensation off the side of her glass with her fingertips.

"What about me?" Piralli tried not to let any sense of defensiveness creep into his voice but knew that he'd failed when he saw the look on Moona's face.

"Are you happy?"

Piralli frowned. This wasn't the usual sort of question that Moona asked. These nights were typically filled with talk about politics, or news from their homeworlds, or the Jedi, or what the new eatery at the market was selling. Anything but stuff like this. Personal stuff. He took a long draw of his drink.

"What's it matter?" he said. "I'm fine. I like my work. I have good friends. That's good enough, isn't it?"

"So that's a 'no'," said Moona, leveling him with a look.

"It's not a no. I'm content. And that's enough for me."

"Is it?" She rapped her fingertips on the bar. "You deserve to be happy too, you know."

Piralli shrugged. "I know."

"Do you?"

He placed his drink on the counter. "What is this, Moona?"

"I just..." She shook her head. "If there's one thing I've learned, Piralli, it's that life's short. Too short to sit here waiting for something to happen. You have to go out and grasp it. Even if it's uncomfortable or scary."

"'Moona the Wise'," said Piralli, with a crooked smile. "Look, you don't need to worry about me. I've got my ship—"

A Sullustan Mark VIII Legacy-class space yacht, with twin cruiser engines that would give even a Jedi Alpha-3 a run for its money. When it was finished, it was going to be beautiful.

"Your ship! You've been working on that heap of junk for years, Piralli!"

He felt his cheeks flush. "Projects like that take time, Moona. Especially if you're doing it properly like I am."

He couldn't deny it—he had been working on the old ship for years, slowly rebuilding it from original parts claimed from salvage or purchased at extortionate prices from the Bonbraks. A Sullustan Mark VIII *Legacy*-class space yacht, with twin cruiser engines that would give even a Jedi Alpha-3 a run for its money. When it was finished, it was going to be beautiful. A true classic. But it was currently sitting in the same dock at the spaceport that it had occupied since he'd first taken ownership of the old wreck to settle an even older debt.

"You said you were going to sail the stars," said Moona.

"And I am," replied Piralli, a little too quickly. "When it's ready. You can't rush these things."

"It's been eight years!"

Piralli shrugged. "It's not that simple."

"Why?"

"It's missing its central processor. Everything else is done."

"But surely you can pick up a processor unit at the market?" said Moona.

Piralli shook his head. "No. It has to be the *right* processor. It's a classic, Moona. You can't just stick any old processor in it and expect it to fly. It's a sensitive machine. A work of art." He sighed. "And besides, it's a very particular type of processor. The shipyards on Sullust only made them for a couple of years. The ship won't fly without it. They're as rare as Boldavian spit-spines these days."

"All right, but how much can an original processor unit be?"

"About two million Republic credits," said Piralli, forlornly.

"Two million!" Every head in the bar turned at the sound of Moona's exclamation. "But that's..."

"Precisely," said Piralli. "A little out of my price range."

"So, what you're saying is the ship is never going to be finished," said Moona.

"I don't know," said Piralli. "I suppose it was never really about flying it. Keth understood." He glanced at the empty seat where his old friend used to sit. "It gave me something to hope for. Something to talk about. And it was nice. I could pretend that one day I'd be able to take that beautiful old yacht out into the skies to explore the galaxy. But things like that don't happen to people like me. I'm a dockworker on Jedha. It was never anything more than a nice dream."

Moona looked pained. "I'm sorry. I didn't mean to poke at old wounds."

Piralli waved her silent. "It's nothing. Like I said, I'm *fine*. Really." He reached for his drink.

Behind them, the door creaked as it swung open, admitting a newcomer to the tapbar. They both twisted in their seats to see who it was. ▸

A *Jedi*.

Piralli shot Moona a look. "We've not had a visitor like that for some time," he said.

"No," said Moona. "We haven't."

The young human approached the bar. She was dressed in brown robes, practical pants and a white tabard. She had smooth brown skin, a golden nose ring, and long black hair tied back in a tight braid. Twin lightsaber hilts hung from holsters on her belt. She carried herself with an easy confidence.

Piralli turned back to his drink. He was all set to ignore her, carry on with his conversation with Moona. Until he heard the young Jedi use his name.

He turned back to see Old Chantho pointing him out to the newcomer. The Jedi smiled and walked over.

"Hello," she said, offering him a little wave. "Piralli?"

Piralli realized his mouth was hanging open. He closed it, clearing his throat. "Umm, yes."

The Jedi beamed. She looked at Moona. "Then you must be Moona?"

Moona narrowed her eyes. "Perhaps."

The Jedi smiled shyly.

"I'm sorry," said Piralli. "Should we know you?"

The Jedi looked momentarily taken aback. "Oh, no. My fault. I should have opened with that, shouldn't I? I'm just a little excited to meet you, that's all."

Piralli and Moona exchanged another glance. "You *are*?"

"I'm Rooper. Rooper Nitani. I'm a Jedi Knight."

"I think we gleaned that much," said Moona, with a wry grin. "What can we do for you, Rooper Nitani?"

"Well… I suppose I should start at the beginning. I'm here to make a pilgrimage to the Holy City, and my former master, Silandra Sho, suggested I drop in here to look you up." She gestured with her arms to encompass the bar. "Silandra thought I'd find you in here. Even after all this time."

Piralli couldn't prevent the laugh that came bubbling out between his lips. "Silandra Sho! She remembered us?"

"Of course, she did!" said Rooper. "She wanted me to say hello, and to ask after someone called Erta, too."

Moona was laughing now, too. "You can tell her that we're all doing fine. Better than fine. And Erta will be delighted to know that a Jedi was asking after her. She won't believe she missed it!"

Rooper seemed to relax. "That's good. Silandra will be pleased. She's told me all about what happened here. The battle, and your friend."

"Keth Cerapath," said Piralli. "He helped her."

"I know. She hasn't forgotten. She'll never forget," said Rooper.

"None of us will," said Moona. "None of us *should*."

She had smooth brown skin, a golden nose ring, and long black hair tied back in a tight braid. Twin lightsaber hilts hung from holsters on her belt. She carried herself with an easy confidence.

"Our aim was to arrest a man named Ullan Yite, the leader of a criminal organization known as the Bright Circle."

They lapsed into silence for a moment.

"Hey, what about Keth's droid, Peethree? Silandra took him when she left," said Piralli, with a chuckle. "Is he still making trouble for everyone, or has he been consigned to the scrap heap yet?"

"Oh, he's still making trouble. *Lots* of trouble. The adventures we've been on these last few years..." said Rooper, smile so wide she revealed her bright white teeth.

"Tell us," said Piralli, pulling out Keth's old stool. "Take the weight off for a minute. Jedha's not going anywhere."

Rooper, still smiling, lowered herself onto the seat. "Silandra said you were welcoming." She shook her head at an inquiring look from Old Chantho. "All right. One story."

"You're sure you don't want a drink," said Moona.

"I'm sure," said Rooper. "So, let me work out where to begin. Me, Silandra and Peethree were in the floating city of Penumbra, which orbits a gas giant in the Tollello system in the Outer Rim."

"So, nowhere impressive then," said Piralli, laughing.

"The place is a den of vice and iniquity," said Rooper. "So you're not far from the truth. We'd managed to infiltrate an illegal deal that was taking place, in which a large stash of smuggled weapons was about to be sold to a pirate group that was planning to use them in a series of raids on the other settlements in the sector."

"So far, so Jedi," said Moona.

"Our aim was to arrest a man named Ullan Yite, the leader of a criminal organization known as the Bright Circle. Our intelligence suggested the whole operation would collapse without him, and the pirates would be rendered toothless without their supplier."

"And Peethree was part of this?" said Piralli. It was hard to believe that the little droid that Keth built was now out amongst the stars helping the Jedi to fight pirates and smugglers.

"He was," said Rooper. "His job was to infiltrate the control systems inside Penumbra and close the blast doors to prevent Yite from escaping to his yacht."

"From your tone, I'm assuming everything didn't go to plan?" asked Piralli.

"Not exactly," said Rooper. "When the moment came to make our move, the blast doors didn't shut. Ullan Yite bolted, and, just as we'd feared, he headed straight for his yacht in the space dock. Silandra and I gave chase, of course, but we could hear Ullan's enforcer droids mustering behind us. We turned to engage them, but before they were in range to attack, the blast doors finally came down, shutting them off."

"So Peethree missed his cue?" said Moona.

"Oh, no," said Rooper, wagging her finger. "He knew exactly what he was doing. Me and Silandra were trapped. Although safe from the enforcer droids, we were stuck behind the blast doors while Ullan Yite got clean away. Well, that's what we thought, anyway. But by the time we cut our way out with our lightsabers, Yite was stuck too. Peethree had sabotaged his yacht. It wouldn't fly. And his enforcer droids were still trapped back in his complex and couldn't come to his aid."

"So you got him?" said Piralli.

"We did. The mission was a

complete success."

"Just not in the way that you'd planned it," said Moona, laughing. "Peethree always did have his own way of doing things."

"That's one way of putting it," said Rooper, rolling her eyes.

Piralli shook his head. "Why *did* he go against the plan though? He must have had a reason."

Rooper grinned. "I think you'd better ask him that yourself." She twisted in her seat, pursing her lips to issue a shrill whistle.

"What...?" Piralli started, but Rooper just gestured towards the door.

A moment later—much to the consternation of the Twinkle Sisters, who were forced to stand back to make way—the hodgepodge droid that was P3-7A came gliding regally through the open doors, responding to Rooper's summons.

Piralli hooted in laughter. The droid looked just the same as he had when Keth had first built him, aside from the addition of several scratches to his paintwork and a handful of new dents. The broad, disc-shaped body, the trailing, segmented appendages, the strange golden head in an ornate cage, mounted on top—they were all just as he remembered them.

Moona was already out of her stool and running over to greet the strange droid like he was an old friend. Which, Piralli reflected, he was.

"Peethree! It's good to see you!" said Moona, wrapping her arms around his bulky middle section.

Lights danced across P3-7A's pitted shell. "Only the pious know the true worth of companionship, for the Living Force binds all things," said the droid, and for once, Piralli sensed no sarcasm in its delivery of the epigram.

Moona stepped out of the way so Piralli could greet P3-7A. The sight of him warmed Piralli's heart but brought back difficult memories of Keth and everything that they had lost, too.

"Welcome back, old friend," said Piralli, patting P3-7A gently. "I hear you've been getting yourself into quite some trouble out there, in the galaxy."

"There is only one truth beneath the stars, and that is the Force," said P3-7A, and this time the sarcasm was dripping. "Yet, know that the Force is a gift, and it is given unto us freely."

A small hatch popped open in his outer casing, revealing a hidden compartment.

Piralli glanced at Rooper, frowning.

"Go on," said Rooper. "Take a look."

Confused, Piralli reached out his hand. There was something fist-sized inside the compartment—something that felt uncannily like...

"A central processor!" said Piralli, withdrawing his hand to reveal the electronic component he'd taken from inside the droid.

Moona was staring at him blankly. "What? You're pulling out the poor droid's guts."

But Rooper was laughing.

The droid looked just the same as he had when Keth had first built him, aside from the addition of several scratches to his paintwork and a handful of new dents

"No!" said Piralli, staring wide-eyed at the device in his hand. "No. It's a central processor from a ship. A Sullustan Mark VIII *Legacy*-class space yacht…" He tried to say something more but the words just stuttered out, incomprehensible.

"What? You mean… *Oh*!" said Moona. "By the Light. It doesn't look like it's worth two million credits!"

"Keep your voice down!" said Piralli, but he was laughing, unable to contain the sheer joy welling up inside of him. "Where did you get this, Peethree?"

"Where there is darkness, the light may one day come to shine," said P3-7A, cryptically.

"Ullan Yite!" said Piralli, realization dawning. He looked at Rooper. "You said he had a yacht. That's why Peethree did what he did, isn't it? That's why you told us that story. Peethree sabotaged the ship by stealing *this*!"

Rooper cleared her throat. "Well, as a Jedi, I could never condone theft of any sort…" She laughed. "But let's just say Peethree knew how this particular component of that seized, illegally obtained vessel could be… *repurposed*." She shrugged. "And besides, you try arguing with him when he has his mind set on something."

Piralli felt tears streaming down his cheeks. Did the little droid know what gift he had given him? This was more than just a piece of impossible-to-find tech. This was *freedom*. It was the fulfillment of a lifelong dream.

It was everything.

Piralli bundled the droid up into an uncomfortable hug. "Oh, Peethree. Thank you. Thank you *so much*. Keth would have been so proud."

P3-7A made an upbeat pipping sound. "All will be remembered in the Force, with kindness."

Yes.

That was it *exactly*.

Kindness.

Keth could never truly be gone, not if even a little of his kindness remained out there in the galaxy. And it did. It remained in the shape of this strange, misshapen droid. A droid that had remembered Piralli after all these years and had come back to find him and bestow on him a gift that would change his life forever.

Moona was beaming at Piralli. She hooked her arm around his shoulders. "You'd better promise to take me, Erta and the kids on a holiday in that grand ship of yours," she said, squeezing him tight. "I'll not have you forgetting about us as you go off to explore the stars."

"How could I?" said Piralli, his voice catching in his throat. "How could I ever forget any of you?"

He glanced at Rooper. "I really don't know what to say," he continued. "This is an amazing gift."

Rooper smiled but shook her head. "Oh, this is all on the droid," she said, jerking her thumb in P3-7A's direction. "I had nothing to do with it."

Piralli laughed. He slipped the processor into his pocket, and then leaned on the bar, raising his voice. "Kradon?"

The Villerandi looked up from his Umbaran companion, curious. "Yes, my friend?"

"Open a cask of your best ale. The good stuff that you keep hidden out the back. I want to buy a round of drinks for my friends." Piralli looked at Moona, and Old Chantho, and the rest of them, all smiling at him happily. "I want to buy a round of drinks for my *family*."

Kradon rose from his seat, gesturing to the Umbaran to stay right where they were. "Of course," he said. "Kradon understands. Kradon understands all too well."

Piralli sat back on his stool. He was surrounded by the people he loved. Friends, both present and those just out of reach.

And for the first time in years, he felt happy.

THE END

COMETH THE HOUR

Author George Mann reveals how his twin childhood obsessions with *Star Wars* and storytelling, and a love of horror movies, led to a career in writing and his arrival in *The High Republic*.

WORDS: MARK NEWBOLD

COMETH THE MANN

A fan of the saga since childhood, George Mann has become increasingly ubiquitous within the *Star Wars* galaxy, writing for IDW Comics' *Star Wars Adventures* as well as the trio of fan-favorite books—*Myths & Fables, Dark Legends* and *The Life Day Treasury*. We sat down with George to find out about his storytelling journey.

***Star Wars Insider*: Can you remember when *Star Wars* first entered your world?**
George Mann: My first experience with *Star Wars* was when my grandad took me to the cinema to see *Star Wars: The Empire Strikes Back* (1980). I was about four years old, and it was one of the first films I saw at the cinema. From that point on I was completely obsessed with it. It fired my imagination as a little kid, but it was seeing R2-D2 that really did it.

After the movies had come and gone I moved onto other things, but for a long time I read the Marvel UK comic reprints, and then as a young adult I got a job in a bookshop and started reading *Star Wars* novels, so it never really went away.

When did you know that you wanted to be a writer?
I always knew. As a kid I made up stories all the time. I'd fold sheets of paper together to make little books and illustrate them myself. I rented a PC when I moved to Sutton Coldfield (a town near Birmingham in the U.K.) to work in a bookshop, but the only software it had on it was a word processor, so I thought to myself, "I might as well write a story." Once I'd started, it reminded me just how much I loved making stories. Working in the bookshop at the time, I was well connected to what was going on in publishing. I was reading a lot too, and after writing a few short stories and making some abortive attempts at writing a novel in order to learn the craft, I decided I wanted to be a professional writer.

My first book, *The Mammoth Encyclopedia of Science Fiction*, was published in 2000, and a couple of years later I had some fiction published in a novella. My first novel was published in 2008. I sent a chunk of another book I'd written to a friend of mine to ask what he thought of it. At the time he was doing some consultancy work for a publisher, and he showed them the manuscript. They came back to me and said, "We've read this, we really like it. If you finish it, we'll publish it." Amazingly, that turned into a multi-book deal, and I had my break.

"As a kid I made up stories all the time. I'd fold sheets of paper together to make little books and illustrate them myself."

I moved into publishing and went to Games Workshop to run the Black Library. I wrote a lot of Doctor Who, including a *War Doctor* novel that was very successful, and I'd reached the point where I was turning away writing work ▶

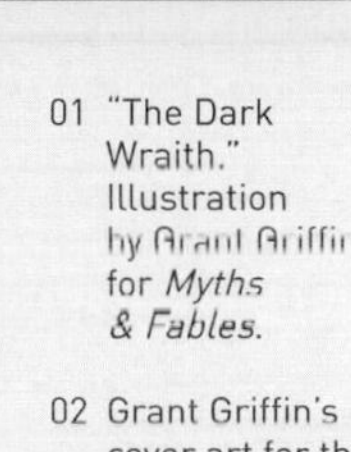

01 "The Dark Wraith." Illustration by Grant Griffin for *Myths & Fables*.

02 Grant Griffin's cover art for the Galaxy's Edge edition of *Myths & Fables*.

03 George Mann.

04 "The Golden One." Illustration by Grant Griffin for the Galaxy's Edge and Target editions of *Myths & Fables*.

05 *Star Wars: Myths and Fables* is a collection of stories "Luke and Leia would have been told at bedtime."

06 *Star Wars: Dark Legends* came from ideas too spooky for *Myths & Fables.*

07 *Star Wars: Life Day Treasury* tells holiday stories from a galaxy far, far away, co-written by Mann and Cavan Scott.

05

06

07

because I couldn't fit it in around my day job. I had a moment of revelation where I asked myself, "What am I doing?!" I took a big pay cut and became a full-time writer, and I've not looked back since.

How did you make the leap to hyperspace writing stories in the galaxy far, far away?
I'd met Michael Siglain of Lucasfilm Publishing at a San Diego Comic-Con with Cavan Scott, and we realized we shared a love of Universal and Hammer horror movies. A few months later I went to New York Comic Con. Cavan was doing *Star Wars* by that point, and he took me along to a party where I met Mike again. I'd written a book called *Wychwood*, which was a spooky, horror, crime novel, and Mike took me to one side and said he'd read it and really loved it. The premise of the book was that a killer was committing murders based on an old Saxon myth, and Mike asked if the mythology in the book was real or made up. When I said, "No, it's all made up for the book," he said, "Wow. Okay, do you want to do that for *Star Wars*?" I nearly fell over (*laughs*)! That's where *Myths & Fables* came from. Mike had this idea for a short story collection, so we started brainstorming ideas and it's gone from there.

08 "Buyer Beware." Illustration by Grant Griffin for *Dark Legends.*

09 "The Dark Mirror." Illustration by Grant Griffin for *Dark Legends.*

How did the premise for *Myths & Fables* develop?
Mike thought it would be great if there were legends and oral stories within the *Star Wars* galaxy, the kind of stories Luke and Leia would have been told at bedtime, like Grimm's fairy tales. Our approach was that we didn't want to disabuse official lore, so while there would be a kernel of truth in each of the stories, the retelling of them over the years might have twisted them slightly. I came up with a slew of suggestions for stories, so I went to the Presidio and sat down with the editor and members of Story Group and we talked through the ideas.

"We realized during our meetings that I'd come up with a lot of dark and spooky ideas."

Myths & Fables is evocative of square-bound illustrated children's books from the late 1970s and early 1980s.
Absolutely, the idea was for a storybook with a fantastic illustration for each story. I remember sitting with books like that as a kid, just staring at the pictures. We were so lucky that Lucasfilm Publishing brought in Grant Griffin to do the artwork. Grant was given detailed outlines, so while I was writing the stories his artwork drafts were coming in. It became a little feedback loop. Quite often I had illustrations on hand for the story I was writing, or was going to write next, on my screen, and it was inspiring. The books wouldn't be what they are without Grant's art, and I think that's a big part of why they have that feel.

08

09

There are also expanded versions of *Myths & Fables,* including one available exclusively at Galaxy's Edge.
That version has six more stories than the standard edition. I'd had an idea for a story about a boy who was taken away and broken by the Emperor and the publishers said, "This is Darth Maul's story. Let's make this boy Darth Maul." I was like, "Whoa, I get to write the legend of Darth Maul's origin story!" As we treat these stories like folklore, there's always "plausible deniability" in terms of official continuity if we do something readers might not like, but so far that's not been the case. The stories have been embraced, but they're definitely to be viewed through that folklore lens.

We realized during our meetings that I'd come up with a lot of dark and spooky ideas, so Mike suggested we finish *Myths* then circle back around and rescue some of those darker ideas for a Halloween book. That's where *Dark Legends* came from.

"*Star Wars* and spooky stories work so well together. It's a very rounded fictional galaxy, so you can tell any kind of story in it."

10

10 "The Witch and the Wookiee." Illustration by Grant Griffin for *Myths & Fables.*

14

11 "An Unwilling Apprentice." Illustration by Grant Griffin for the *Star Wars* Galaxy's Edge: *Myths & Fables* edition.

Did you enjoy the collaborative process of developing ideas with the Lucasfilm team?
I loved it. Writing a book is quite a personal experience. It's just you and a keyboard. Writing for comics is a collaborative exercise, as you're writing a script for an artist, and it's the same with audio. I've done both, but writing *Star Wars* is more collaborative, and I like that about it. Story Group live and breathe *Star Wars*. The stories always get better when you get good input from creative people, and they were very generous in terms of ideas but also in taking my ideas onboard and being happy to let me run with stuff.

I feel like I've been able to contribute something to a galaxy that's given me so much as a fan for years. That's the wonderful thing about it. I've created some characters and told some stories that have given other people joy, hopefully in the same way I get joy from reading other people's stories and watching *Star Wars* on the screen. That's a heart-warming feeling.

In recent years *Star Wars* has embraced Halloween. As a horror fan, that must have been huge fun to bring to fruition.
It was brilliant. *Star Wars* and spooky stories work so well together. It's a very rounded fictional galaxy, so you can tell any kind of story in it, be that romance, espionage, an action adventure, or a spooky story. It's built in—you've got Force spirits, you've got monstrous Sith with dark magic, Darth Vader as the bogeyman. It all fits so well. *Star Wars* has always had this tradition. It's right there in *Empire*, with Luke in the swamp on Dagobah and the Force-visions of his own face in Vader's mask. It's got that tone, the misty swamplands where monsters lurk.

There's a big tonal gear change between *Dark Legends* and *The Life Day Treasury*, which you co-wrote with Cavan Scott. Where did that idea come from?

PLOTTING EASTER EGGS

Among the joys to be found in *Star Wars* literature, references to characters and places across multiple books and comics provide eagle-eyed readers with a great deal of fun. Working alongside other writers in the *Star Wars* stable has provided George Mann with numerous opportunities to scatter Easter eggs throughout his work.

"It's a lot of fun to do, planting seeds," says Mann. "Cavan Scott and I were both working on multiple *Star Wars* projects, so what we ended up doing was throwing in stuff that we'd each later reference. There's a story in *Life Day Treasury* called 'The Kindling,' about a Twi'lek colony and their winter traditions and folklore. We called the planet Aaloth, and when Cavan was writing *Tempest Runner*, he made that planet Lourna Dee's homeworld.

"There are Easter eggs in there for things that are already out, and things that might come out in the future," Mann continues. "I wrote a Drengir story for the Target edition of *Dark Legends*, and that came out before *Light of the Jedi*. No one knew that the Drengir was in any way related to *The High Republic*. It's just a story about a plant-based monster on Batuu called the Drengir. Michael Siglain was teasing people before *The High Republic* even launched, saying, 'We've already put a story out there and no one's realized!' That was a lot of fun as well."

Cavan pitched the idea of a Life Day book to Mike Siglain, and he suggested that as I was already doing this series of books, we should work together on it. Cavan and I have written a lot of material together previously, including *Doctor Who*, *Sherlock Holmes*, and original stuff, so we've built up a good level of trust between us. We both love folklore, we both love Christmas ghost stories, and that was the approach we wanted to take with *Life Day Treasury*.

We started off by asking ourselves, "What kind of stories do we want to tell?" There was a Christmas ghost story, a winter truce story that riffed on the football match between the English and the Germans during World War One, a story about Ewoks and monsters, and we wanted a romance set around new year. Obviously, we had to have a Wookiee story.

We spent a couple of days talking through the stories, working out the ideas behind them, and divided them up, writing five stories each. We each wrote a first draft and then swapped and rewrote each other's work, polishing each story and making them better. It never felt like any of the stories were either mine or Cav's—we've looked at the book since and neither of us can remember who wrote which one. It was a very pure collaboration, and a great experience.

Your first stories for *The High Republic* were young readers books, and now you'll be playing a larger role in the writing of Phase Two. How did you join the ranks of the original team of five writers?

I'd read all *The High Republic* documents and background material for the Drengir story in *Dark Legends*, and I'd been reading the novels as a fan, so when Mike Siglain asked if I'd be interested in writing *Showdown at the Fair*, showing events from Burryaga's point of view during *The Rising Storm*, I jumped at the chance. I've already dipped my toe into the era with short stories in *Dark Legends* and *Life Day Treasury*, as well as the two young readers picture books (including *The Battle for Starlight*), and I can't wait to immerse myself more fully in those stories. I'm a huge fan of what the team has created, and I'm really excited to be a part of it going forward. It's been a lot of fun to get involved.

12

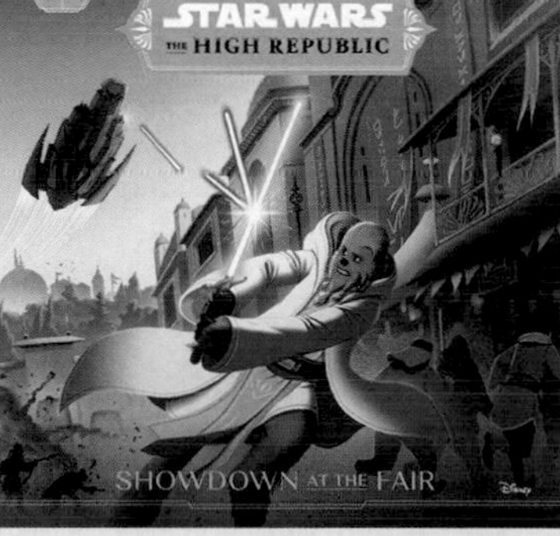

13

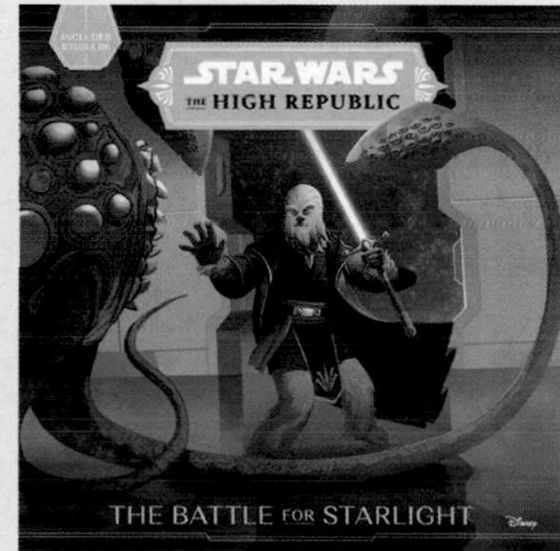

12 13 George Mann's first forays into *The High Republic* include *Showdown at the Fair* and *The Battle For Starlight*. Both illustrations by Petur Antonsson.

Zoraida Córdova, Tessa Gratton, Lydia Kang, and George Mann discuss their arrival on the galactic landscape of a longer time ago.

WORDS: AMY RICHAU

JOINING THE QUEST

***Star Wars: The High Republic* returns this fall with new stories set a long time ago, before the events in Phase I, and a group of new authors are joining the original writing team. Zoraida Córdova, Tessa Gratton, Lydia Kang, and George Mann spoke with *Star Wars Insider* to discuss what excites them about writing for the newest era in *Star Wars*.**

***Star Wars Insider*: Can you remember when you first learned about *The High Republic* and what your initial expectations were as a *Star Wars* fan?**
Lydia Kang: I'd heard murmurings about it in 2020 but didn't really sit up and pay attention until Charles Soule's book, *The Light of the Jedi*, was released. I remember thinking, "How are they going to do this?!"
Zoraida Córdova: I first heard about it during a convention where they began teasing Project Luminous. This great endeavor, it was so exciting.
Tessa Gratton: Justina Ireland and I are really good friends, and I first heard about it from her. I think she had a really hard time not telling me anything about it anytime sooner because she knew I'd been a *Star Wars* fan for my whole life.
George Mann: It's a very similar story for me. I was with my friend Cavan Scott at San Diego Comic-Con the night he was invited to take part in the initiative, but he wasn't allowed to tell me anything about it. Later, I'd get these little video calls from him, saying "I'm at Skywalker Ranch. I can't tell you what we're talking about, but *I'm at Skywalker Ranch!* And I'm bringing back a pen!"

How did you find out you were going to be a part of *The High Republic* writing team?
TG: Justina told me she wanted to write her Phase II book with me. I really can't say much about the story itself, but it really hits a lot of my favorite things to write about as a YA author.
ZC: I'd missed an initial email from Lucasfilm Publishing, and eventually spoke to Mike Siglain about writing an adult novel. I had a feeling of what I wanted the book to be, but I didn't know who the main characters were yet. My story includes all of my favorite things about *Star Wars*: action, romance, and the push and pull between the things you can't have and the things you can. That eternal battle between good and evil that *Star Wars* really is.
GM: I'd been asked to write a story that tied into the High Republic for a special edition of *Dark Legends* (a short-story anthology published by Disney Lucasfilm Press in 2020). So, even before I'd read Charles ▸

01 (Opposite page) Zoraida Córdova, Tessa Gratton, Lydia Kang, and George Mann.

02 *Convergence*, by Zoraida Córdova, published by Del Rey and on sale November 15.

Soule's book, I'd been able to read the 200 page High Republic bible that outlines what they were doing with the first tranche of stories. And then the requests to write some more kept rolling in, with another story for *Life Day Treasury as well as other children's books.*

I had no hesitation at any point in the process. Definitely not.

LK: My agent called asking if I'd like to work on the High Republic, and after getting over the shock my initial thought was the same as I'd had when they asked me to write a short story for one of the *From a Certain Point of View* anthologies, which was, "I can't do that!" It was such a huge honor I was overwhelmed, and really hesitant. And both times my husband said, "You need to just stop now and hit the "yes" button."

03

04

STAR WARS
MYTHS & FABLES
WRITTEN BY
GEORGE MANN

05

06

03 Tessa Gratton contributed a short story to the *Star Wars: Stories of Jedi and Sith* anthology.

04 *Myths & Fables* by George Mann.

05 Zoraida Córdova's Galaxy's Edge novel, *A Crash of Fate.*

06 *Path of Deceit* by Tessa Gratton and Justina Ireland, published by Disney Lucasfilm Press and on sale October 4.

You've all written at least one other *Star Wars* story. Can you talk about how your work on *The High Republic* has differed from those previous projects?

TG: I wrote my tale for *Stories of Jedi and Sith* before I wrote anything for *The High Republic.* The publisher wanted me to dip my toes into the galaxy with a short story before throwing me into the deep end of a *The High Republic* novel. And I'm really glad they did. Pitching the idea for the short story was a very different experience. I had to work much harder on *The High Republic* pitch because I had to know exactly what the novel was going to be.

ZC: My experience writing *Star Wars: Galaxy's Edge: A Crash of Fate* was quite similar to writing for *The High Republic,* because it tied into the larger narrative of the theme park. I learned about Batuu

"We've been given a whole new sandbox to work in with both Galaxy's Edge and the High Republic era. There's so much more to play with."
Zoraida Córdova

07

in the same way that I have been learning about the Quest of the Jedi phase, through massive documents packed with character profiles. We've been given a whole new sandbox to work in with both Galaxy's Edge and the High Republic era. There's so much more to play with.

GM: With the myths and legends stuff I've written, it was very open-ended in that those were the legends that were told *within* the *Star Wars* galaxy, so I had all this flexibility to tell these wild stories and be really creative with them. I'd assumed that *The High Republic* experience was going to be the opposite of that because there was already this weight of existing material with all the Phase I books, but actually it wasn't. Yes, there was a lot to bear in mind and you had to get the characterizations right, but there was still a huge amount of room in which to add your own voice to the story, to add something new to the worlds we've been developing, and what you want to do with the characters.

LK: I remember watching everyone doing their thing and trying to figure out how I was going to piece my project ►

07 *Quest For The Hidden City* by George Mann. Published by Disney Lucasfilm Press and on sale November 1.

READING *THE HIGH REPUBLIC*

The new authors reflect on their initial experiences of *The High Republic* as readers and reveal their favorite Phase I characters and storylines.

Zoraida: I read Phase I in chronological order, starting with *Light of the Jedi*. For me, the highlight was the storyline between Elzar Mann, Avar Kriss, and Stellan Gios. That little love-triangle-that's-not-really-a-love-triangle, but is. I became deeply invested in that. And Elzar Mann is my favorite character. He is a gentleman and a scholar. I love him so much.

Lydia: I read the three adult novels one after the other, and then delved into the YA books, then the middle grade stories. I loved Reath Silas in Claudia Grays' book, *Into the Dark*. He just loves being in libraries and researching things. He's sort of reluctant to be out there where things are scary. I thought, "Oh, I get him. He's like me." And I want to give a shout out to Geode, who's maybe one of my absolute favorite characters of all time.

Tessa: I've been reading them in order, but I've been like that my whole life. I couldn't read them out of order, it would just ruin my entire experience. I'm a YA writer at heart so the YA books are my favorites. I really loved *Out of the Shadows* by Justina Ireland. I enjoyed all of the hyperspace science and how things work, and I loved the main character, Silvestri Yarrow. I also really liked Xylan Graf. He is sort of a bad guy, but I'm very interested in the Graf family's history and what they'd been doing.

George: I think what Daniel José Older did with the Padawan team in the IDW *The High Republic Adventures* comics was so cute, and the relationship between Keeve Trennis and Sskeer in the Marvel comics was fantastically done. Watching Keeve evolve from a freshly minted Knight to this fully fledged, fully capable character was a great journey. I think they are probably my favorite team.

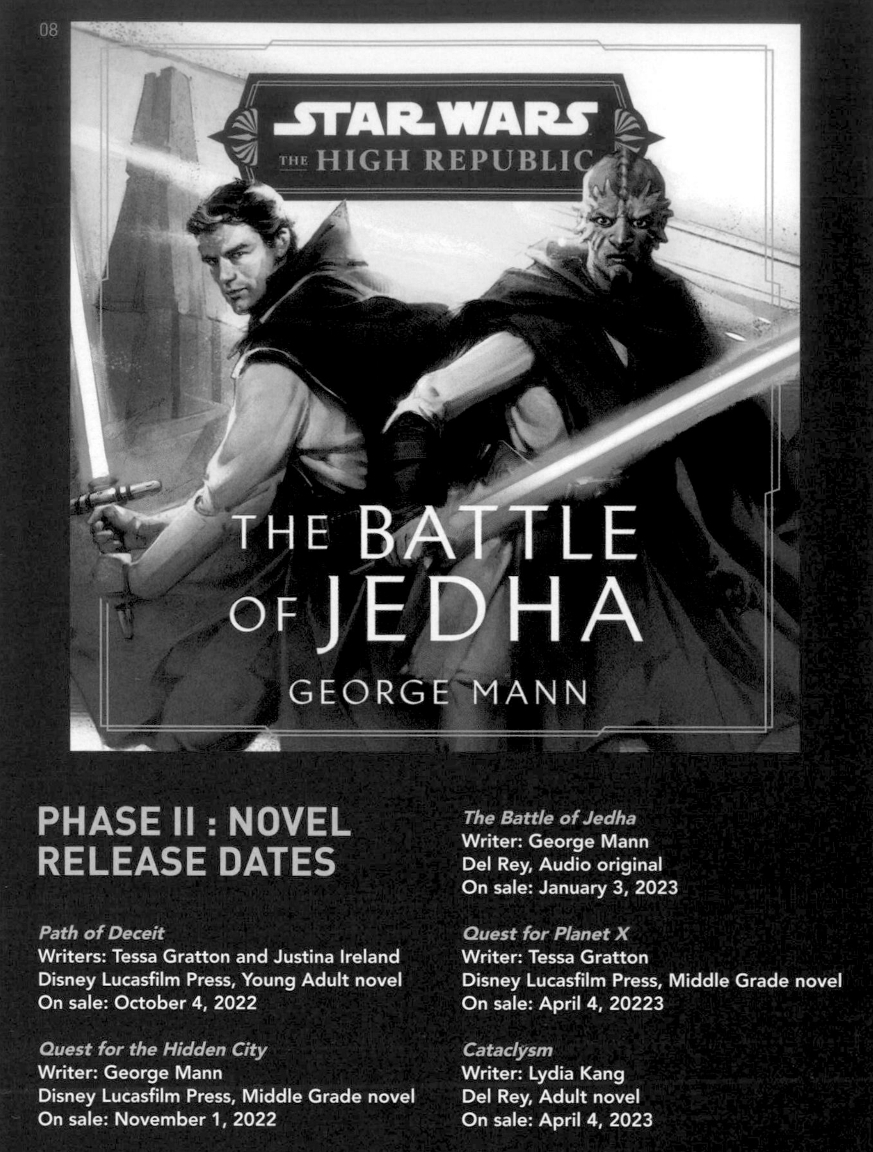

PHASE II : NOVEL RELEASE DATES

Path of Deceit
Writers: Tessa Gratton and Justina Ireland
Disney Lucasfilm Press, Young Adult novel
On sale: October 4, 2022

Quest for the Hidden City
Writer: George Mann
Disney Lucasfilm Press, Middle Grade novel
On sale: November 1, 2022

Convergence
Writer: Zoraida Córdova
Del Rey, Adult novel
On sale: November 15, 2022

The Battle of Jedha
Writer: George Mann
Del Rey, Audio original
On sale: January 3, 2023

Quest for Planet X
Writer: Tessa Gratton
Disney Lucasfilm Press, Middle Grade novel
On sale: April 4, 20223

Cataclysm
Writer: Lydia Kang
Del Rey, Adult novel
On sale: April 4, 2023

Path of Vengeance
Writer: Cavan Scott
Disney Lucasfilm Press, Young Adult novel
On sale: May 2, 2023

▶ together. It was mind-blowingly different to juggle all those different storylines, where everything was super woven together. It was really intimidating. When I wrote "The Right-Hand Man" for the anthology, I got over my fear of writing it through my work as a physician. I wrote it from the perspective of a health care professional, like the medical droid from *The Empire Strikes Back* (1980), 2-1B; since it was a language I was familiar with, I knew I could do that. Jumping from something that was very comfortable to this has been a huge transition, but it's been fantastic. And working with everybody on *The High Republic* team has been so wonderful.

08 Cover for *The Battle for Jedha*, an audio original book, written by George Mann.

"Working with everybody on *The High Republic* team has been so wonderful."
Lydia Kang

Phase II of *The High Republic* is set 150 years before Phase I. Did you find that step back in time challenging?
GM: I'm always looking for angles where I can add something interesting to *Star Wars*, how I can give something back to it, so my driver with Quest for the Jedi was very much to create new characters. I knew where the galaxy was heading, the direction of travel for the Republic and where the novel was going to end up, but that still left huge amounts of room to tell new stories.
TG: I find it really exciting. Before I start writing anything,
I need to know where it ends. In this case we know where characters are and where the Republic is 150 years after our stories. So, in a lot of ways, we have a shape that we are filling out. It's sort of a foundation that we've been building.
ZC: One of the exciting challenges as a writer has been understanding what was happening in the galaxy at that point. So, if I wanted to put in an Easter egg, I had to consider if this or that planet been discovered by the Republic yet? It's exploratory writing as much as it is anything, because you don't know what you can't do until you've written it.
LK: I'm fascinated by how things change over time in the history of the *Star Wars* galaxy. One of the things I found really freeing and exciting about this time period was that, knowing where everything

was going to be 150 years from now, we were able to take a step back and ask, "Well, how are things different?" For example, the politics and the Jedi are not the same, and we really got to sink our teeth into that and question how those differences might have shaped our characters and stories.

Why do you think that *The High Republic* project has resonated with so many *Star Wars* fans?

ZC: Because it has expanded the galaxy in such a way that there are still so many things to discover. Even though there are familiar archetypes that everybody loves, it feels new. And there's so much to anchor into and to root for.

TG: *The High Republic* is doing so much work with the Jedi in particular. The Jedi are extremely specific in the movies—we know what they think they are. What we're answering is the question of how they got that way and how the Jedi remained so important for so long? That seems like a fundamental question that the saga has been asking for a long time. *The High Republic* is answering that question.

LK: It makes sense that *Star Wars* should go in this direction. We've already had so many stories building on the lore of the movies, fleshing out this huge, huge galaxy across big chunks of time. Now we have *The High Republic*—the prequel to the prequels: it's different, yet very familiar.

GM: One of the things I love about *Star Wars* is that it's like a myth for the modern age. If you think of *Star Wars* as Homer's *The Odyssey*, what we're working on is *The Iliad*. It's another mythic cycle within the same framework, telling an earlier story that sheds light on one we already know. I think *Rogue One: A Star Wars Story* (2016) is a brilliant example of where that happens in the movies, and for me *Rogue One* makes *A New Hope* (1977) even better. That's what we're trying to do with Phase II of *The High Republic*. We're trying to tell a new cycle of stories that gives you a perspective on the Jedi and the Force in a way that you don't get from the movies, but still feels as though it's part of that galaxy. That's the attraction for me as a fan going into *The High Republic*.

"We're trying to tell a new cycle of stories that gives you a perspective on the Jedi and the Force in a way that you don't get from the movies."
George Mann

09

09 *The Nameless Terror* from Dark Horse comics is a miniseries written by George Mann with art by Eduardo Mello. Issue #1 cover by Ornella Savarese.

ZORAIDA CÓRDOVA

THE FORCE OF FANTASY

Zoraida Córdova, author of *Star Wars: A Crash of Fate* and *The High Republic: Convergence*, tells *Insider* about her passion for crafting stories of love and redemption, and finding a home in the *Star Wars* galaxy.

WORDS: CHELSEA ZUKOWSKI

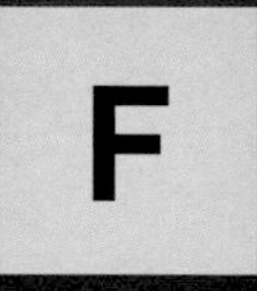

For fantasy author Zoraida Córdova, the worlds of *Star Wars* are ripe for spinning fantasy fairy tales. "What is the Force if not fantasy enduring?" she suggests. "This idea that you have a powerful thing that connects every single living being, that some people are in tune with and can wield great power through. And the Jedi are space wizards; that is also fantasy," she adds.

It's on the warring planets of Eiram and E'ronoh that Córdova set her latest *Star Wars* fantasy stage in *Convergence*, part of *The High Republic*'s second phase of storytelling, and she drew on a certain Shakespearean influence in its tale of longtime enemies turned star-crossed lovers—a prince and a princess who hail from cultures rich with their own unique histories and mythos. "It's *Romeo and Juliet* in space, except less tragic," Córdova jokes. "We have these two planets at war, but they're also neighbors, so shouldn't they have something in common? ►

01 Author Zoraida Córdova reading her Batuu-set novel *A Crash of Fate* at Galaxy's Edge.

02

"What is the Force if not fantasy enduring?"

The Force Awakens

Córdova's big break into writing *Star Wars* came when a representative from publisher Del Rey contacted her agent asking if the author would be interested in penning a short story. She said she wondered how they knew about her love of *Star Wars*, but then remembered a moment of social media stardom.

"I'm pretty sure I had tweeted something very naughty about Poe Dameron, and it had gone mini viral. Sometimes Twitter is good for something," she jokes.

▶ What are the things that made their societies? To me, it's their beliefs. And belief is oftentimes shaped by geography, by agriculture, and by questions like 'Why are we here?' and 'What do we believe in?'

Córdova's approach to fantasy storytelling is a key part of her signature style, crafting compelling and complicated characters, inventing and expanding the mythos of the fictional worlds she plays in, while infusing her stories with nods to her own Latin American heritage and culture. All these themes are evident in her *Star Wars* novels, short stories, and other fantasy works like *The Inheritance of Orquídea Divina* and *Incendiary*.

Seeing Is Believing

Her passion for fantasy and fairy tales is also something Córdova can trace back to her childhood, specifically to the pivotal moment where she discovered her love of reading and writing, which didn't happen until her early teens.

"I knew I loved fairy tales, and I loved magic and fantasy TV shows," the author explains, "But I was never given the kind of fiction to read where I could see myself as somebody exploring magic or going into outer space and searching for new worlds."

That all changed when she was given an extra-credit assignment and told to pick any book from the library and read it. Córdova chose *In the Forests of the Night* by Amelia Atwater-Rhodes, a vampire story written and published when Atwater-Rhodes was 15 and Córdova was 13.

Córdova was captivated with the idea of a young author who was so close to her own age, and soon devoured the book's sequel before moving on to seek out the work of other fantasy writers.

02 Córdova's short story for the anthology *From a Certain Point of View* featured a plot to steal the *Millennium Falcon*.

"I became enamored with urban fantasy and the idea of the magical world sitting in sync with the real world," she says. "And, of course, I was a Disney Princess girl growing up. I'm pretty sure watching *The Little Mermaid* (1989) on repeat was how I first learned to speak English before we emigrated to the United States."

Another common thread in many of Córdova's stories is romance—a foundational component in both of her full-length *Star Wars* novels, *Convergence* and *A Crash of Fate*. "*Star Wars* would be very different without the central love story of Anakin Skywalker and Padmé Amidala, Luke and Leia's parents," Córdova asserts. "Their love was so powerful it changed the literal trajectory of the galaxy. Love is... not to be super 'woo-woo,' but love is *the thing*. Love is the force that drives every decision. It's behind a lot of the choices we make, not just for survival but for the survival of others. It might be idealistic to think, 'oh, love can save everything,' but because *Star Wars* is about hope, I'll allow myself to be a little idealistic."

"*Star Wars* would be very different without the central love story."

03 Córdova focused on Asajj Ventress for her "The Lost Nightsister" short story.

Love, War, and Peace

The theme of love is very much present in Córdova's *Star Wars* stories, and it's a key aspect driving the story and characters in *Convergence*—love for another person, love for one's people and culture, love for one's home planet, and love and hope for peace.

While there are multiple points of view in *Convergence*, the novel chiefly follows Princess Xiri Albaran of E'ronoh, Phan-tu Zenn of Eiram, Jedi Knight Gella Nattai, and son of the chancellor Axel Greylark. Xiri and Phan-tu are the betrothed heirs of this tale who are desperately hoping their union will also bring their planets together for some semblance of peace and an end to the Forever War. Though hailing from longtime enemies, their love for their people overrides their unexplainable disdain.

"With Eiram and E'ronoh, you have planets that have been at war for an eternity—what is the thing that is going to save them?" Córdova says of her *The High Republic* novel. "It's going to be a union between these two people that eventually becomes something more. That only makes things stronger because now they have more to lose. There's that very fine line where you can love something but not want to possess it," she adds. "That's where the Jedi have to find their balance in my story. I think that's a very, very interesting story to tell, as people will find out with my girl Gella in *Convergence*. It's like a Jedi myth or legend where I talk about the Force and what it is the Jedi are in search of."

Convergence takes place within the wider narrative of Lucasfilm Publishing's hugely ambitious *The High Republic* initiative, so how did Córdova adapt to writing within a shared *Star Wars* vision?

"Working on *The High Republic* was very cool. It's always a fun ▸

Zoraida Córdova's *Star Wars* Stories

From a Certain Point of View
Short story:
"You Owe Me a Ride"
Anthology
Published by Del Rey, 2017

Star Wars: A Crash of Fate
Young-adult novel
Published by
Disney Lucasfilm Press, 2019

The Clone Wars: Stories of Light and Dark
Short story:
"The Lost Nightsister"
Anthology
Published by
Disney Lucasfilm Press, 2020

The High Republic: Convergence
Novel
Published by Del Rey, 2022

"There are a million stories still to be told."

exercise jumping into something that has so many moving parts," she says. "And there was room to play and to develop the stories we wanted to tell, specifically keeping in sync with Lydia Kang, because her book came after mine."

Kang's novel *Cataclysm* is the penultimate book in *The High Republic* Phase II, acting as a sequel of sorts to the events of *Convergence* and *The Battle of Jedha* while setting up the concluding novel, *Path of Vengeance* by Cavan Scott. Córdova and Kang spent a lot of time texting each other while they were drafting their stories, checking each other's notes for opportunities to mention certain characters and make sure their voices matched from book to book.

"We had to figure out how to make our ideas fit and how they would fit into the grander scheme of things," Córdova explains. "So, I really had to dig deep and make sure I understood my characters, how I saw Axel, and Gella, and Phan-tu and Xiri; that this was the story I wanted for them."

The Tatooine Sandbox

Córdova's first entry into the sandbox of *Star Wars* storytelling came in the short story anthology *Star Wars: From a Certain Point of View*. In her tale, "You Owe Me a Ride," she wove a drama around the Tonnika sisters and their thwarted plans to steal the *Millennium Falcon* in order to get

04 Zoraida Córdova.

03 Zoraida Córdova at Galaxy's Edge.

far away from Tatooine—and the author admits to being intimidated at the prospect of putting pen to paper.

"It was interesting going back to *Star Wars: A New Hope* (1977) and this 30-second clip of the Tonnika sisters," says Córdova. "But it took me a while to get comfortable with having permission to insert my own voice and my own point of view of what might have happened during that time period."

The author returned for the book's sequel, *From a Certain Point of View: The Empire Strikes Back*, for which Córdova wrote an internal monologue for Boba Fett in the scene where he met Darth Vader. "I went back and watched every instance Boba Fett appeared in the prequels and in *Star Wars: The Clone Wars* (2008-2020)," she reveals. "Seeing how this angry young boy became this ruthless bounty hunter, I wanted to show a little bit of that internal conflict he has."

For "The Lost Nightsister" in The *Clone Wars: Stories of Light and Dark*, Córdova had the daunting task of getting into the mind of Asajj Ventress, a Nightsister of Dathomir and former Sith apprentice to Count Dooku. "That was really interesting, and very dark for a middle-grade story," she laughs. "The challenge there was showing all the dark things in a way that would resonate with a younger reader so that they could understand what was happening."

Córdova has also found plenty of room to infuse her own creative voice in her *Star Wars* stories, and the themes that engage her as a writer.

"I like to think about how the *Star Wars* galaxy works," says the writer. "It's expansive; there are thousands and thousands of species and there are a million stories still to be told. In the back of my head, I'm always imagining all of my stories lead back to *A New Hope*; it all leads back to that original vision. Whether it's Izzy in *A Crash of Fate* or even Gella and Axel in *Convergence*, it's about people figuring out where they belong in the galaxy, where and what their home is, and what they are willing to do to protect it."

As a kid, Córdova never imagined having the opportunity to contribute to the *Star Wars* galaxy with stories that resonate with fans of all ages and experiences. "It's not just having the creative freedom, it's being able to take part in a world that means so much to so many people," she concludes. "*Star Wars* is for everyone. It always was, and it always will be. I just can't wait to keep on playing in this sandbox."

LYDIA KANG
THE MAGIC OF MYTHMAKING

Star Wars: The High Republic author Lydia Kang reminisces on her journey from doctor to author and adding a personal touch to the saga.

WORDS: CHELSEA ZUKOWSKI

The importance of diversity and representation in _Star Wars_ cannot be overstated. _The High Republic_ continues to be lauded as the most diverse era of _Star Wars_ seen so far, and that diversity is reflected in the writing talent. Lydia Kang joined the publishing initiative in its second phase with her novel _Star Wars: The High Republic: Cataclysm_, released on April 4, 2023, by Random House Worlds, and she had tears in her eyes when she first saw its cover.

"I couldn't believe that there was an Asian boy in a *Star Wars* book, and that I was able to write his story," says the author. "It was the best thing. It felt so special."

The cover featured Republic Chancellor Kyong Greylark's son and all-around bad boy Axel Greylark carrying a blaster and a strangely familiar lightsaber. The novel is a sequel to Zoraida Córdova's *The High Republic: Convergence*, with whom Kang worked closely. "Zoraida and I knew that Axel was going to be coded Korean," Kang says. "It was Zoraida who came up with Axel's name, which I loved. It's very rock and roll. Lucasfilm and the story architects had the vision to bring diversity to the forefront in *The High Republic*," she adds. "There's so much diversity on our single planet, so it makes sense to think that the galaxy far, far away is also going to be not just species-diverse but human-diverse as well."

"I couldn't believe that there was an Asian boy in a *Star Wars* book, and that I was able to write his story."

Kang recalls her amazement when Rose Tico and her sister Paige showed up on screen in the opening moments of *Star Wars: The Last Jedi*.

"Seeing those characters, who looked like they could've been my cousins, felt really monumental and was a big deal to me, and I know it was for other people too," she says.

A FAMILY TRADITION

Like many people around the world during the past 47 years, Kang grew up watching *Star Wars*, and it was her father who took her to see *A New Hope* when she was six years old. While she doesn't totally remember the experience, she does have "a very vivid memory of Luke Skywalker in his X-wing fighter, wearing those yellow-tinted googles." She also recalls the stress she felt watching ▸

01 *Star Wars: The High Republic* author Lydia Kang.

02

Besides Axel, there are two more characters in *Cataclysm* that, for Kang, signal a personal connection to the galaxy of *Star Wars*—Chancellor Kyong Greylark and the people of the planet Pipyyr.

"Zoraida asked me what Axel's mother's name should be, and the first thing that popped out of my mouth was my mother's name," Kang reveals. "We used one of the syllables of my mother's Korean name, because I look at Kyong Greylark as this indomitable force. She's everything; she's creating the Republic as they speak. She is incredibly skilled in these drawing rooms around Coruscant. She is always put together so perfectly, and that's totally my mom, to a T."

In *Cataclysm*, Kyong Greylark also embodies themes such as parent-child relationships and the consequences of striving for personal and professional perfection.

"She's a parent, and she struggled with parenthood. She's not perfect, and that's not so much a reflection on my mom; that's probably more a reflection on me," Kang admits. "The struggle that I have is being a working parent and wondering if I'm spreading myself too thin. Am I doing enough for my kids, like being there enough, but am I also successful in my career?"

But with Kyong Greylark, Kang is also tipping her hat to her mother, whom she calls "a Wonder Woman who came to the United States not speaking a lick of English.

► him take the fateful shot that blew up the Death Star. After that intense movie-going experience, Kang reveals that she and her family watched the *Star Wars* movies all the time, especially when they came on television during the holidays. And every time a new movie came out, her family was there in the theater. "*Star Wars* is woven into the culture of this American life that I've grown up in," she says.

During the past two years and more than a dozen books later, *The High Republic* has garnered readership across the globe, with fans latching onto dynamic, messy characters like Axel.

"I have noticed there are a lot of Axel fans, and that makes me so happy," Kang smiles. "He's such a troublemaker. But he's the character you just sort of love to scream about."

03

04

02 The cover of *Star Wars: The High Republic: Cataclysm* by Lydia Kang.

03 Concept art of Kyong Greylark.

04 Lydia Kang at *Star Wars* Celebration Europe 2023.

05

05 Lydia Kang (third from right) with other *The High Republic* creatives and *The Acolyte* creator and executive producer Leslye Headland (fifth from the left) at *Star Wars* Celebration Europe 2023.

06 Concept art of Axel Greylark, Kang's lead character in *Cataclysm*.

06

"*Star Wars* is woven into the culture of this American life that I've grown up in."

"Mom had her first child after getting married here; not knowing how to drive, not having any friends, not having any family, and just navigating her way through a foreign land," Kang reflects. "And she did it with grace and strength, and I'll admire her to the ends of the Earth for that."

Kyong Greylark is among Kang's favorite characters. The author and part-time practicing physician had huge fun exploring what was most important to Kyong as the High Republic chancellor and as a mother of a young man who had lost his way.

"Her story came so naturally because I knew from the very, very beginning what her struggle was," says Kang. "I knew how she was going to get through it, and I was able to explore what happens when you peel away the finery. What kind of person is left at the end of the day when the makeup and the jewels come off?"

In *Cataclysm*, Kang also paid homage to her furry companion who "basically sat next to me throughout the writing of every *Star Wars* anything that I've ever written." The Pipyyrians are named after her dog, Piper, a Shih Tzu-poodle mix who Kang says looks like an Ewok. The planet Pipyyr also offered Kang a chance to flex some of her medical expertise, especially as it pertains to the effects of altitude sickness.

"It was fun for me to be able to touch on a couple of medical things in *Cataclysm*," she says. "When I wrote about the altitude issues on Pipyyr or anytime there was an injury, I got to really sit with the idea and ask myself, 'How am I going to make this work?'"

WRITING IS A PASSION

The writing that brought Kang to Lucasfilm Publishing's attention included young-adult science fiction and adult historical fiction, including *Control* and *A Beautiful Poison*. She also co-authored historical nonfiction like *Quackery: A Brief History of the Worst Ways to Cure Everything* and *Patient Zero: A Curious History of the World's Worst Diseases*, utilizing her professional experience as a medical practitioner. Prior to taking up her writing career, Kang had loved science and biology so much that she became a doctor of internal medicine.

"When I was in college, I liked biology and helping ▸

RELATABILITY

Lydia Kang on how the characters in *Star Wars: The High Republic: Cataclysm* have recognizable personal challenges that are very down to Earth.

"In *Star Wars* stories, oftentimes you're dealing with characters who are at vastly different levels of development, whether that's emotional or professional, if that's what you want to call being a Jedi," says the author. "You've got Padawans, you've got younglings, you've got masters, and you've also got humans and other characters who are just dealing with different things based on where they are in life. And there's always a challenge that comes at that level that nobody else has to deal with. Looking at Xiri and Phan-tu (of E'ronoh and Eiram), they're newly married. They're navigating what it's like to be in a relationship where there's so much on the line, not just personally, but between two enormous worlds. And then there's Yaddle's challenge of mentoring a really, really gifted youngling, because there's nothing easy for the masters either. It's the same thing with Char-Ryl-Roy and Creighton Sun and Aida Forte, a Knight, and Enya Keen, who's a Padawan.

Each of them has a very specific struggle that they deal with because of the gifts and the knowledge and the wisdom that they have, but also the situation that they've been put in."

07

"There's so much of the human struggle in *Star Wars*, and the desires and hopes that we all have."

people out, so medicine seemed like a very natural extension of where I needed to go," she explains.The catalyst (also the name of Kang's sequel to *Control*) that connected her career in medicine to writing came after an essay she'd written about patient care was published in a medical journal. That led her to write more poetry and essays on the subject and inspired her to expand on her ideas in a young-adult novel.

"I remember thinking, I just want to try to do this; it sounds so exciting and fun to try to write an actual novel," says Kang. "And so, I did; I wrote a book, and I wrote it in a month. It wasn't very good."

However, Kang says that first attempt "lit the flame" of excitement for novel writing. "And once the flame was lit, I just kept going," she says.

Her entry point into writing for the *Star Wars* galaxy came in *From a Certain Point of View: The Empire Strikes Back* anthology, with a story about 2-1B, the medical droid who was first seen on Hoth and again on the medical frigate in *Star Wars: The Empire Strikes Back*. "I know exactly what it means to take care of somebody who's hurt on multiple levels," she states. "So, I wrote 'Right Hand Man,' which is from the perspective of 2-1B while he is attaching Luke's cybernetic hand.

"Luke goes from being so heartbroken at finding out that Darth Vader is his father, and then at the very end of the movie, after he gets his new hand, he looks out the window with Leia and he has an expression of peace on his face. And how did he go from being crushed to having hope? He was hanging out with the medical droid!" Kang smiles.

THE PHILOSOPHY OF SURVIVAL

Star Wars has always felt like a straightforward fight between good and evil, but, especially with recent projects like *The High Republic* and *Star Wars: Andor* the saga has explored the gray areas of the spectrum between right and wrong.

"Fighting for whatever cause is messy; there is so much more nuance in life and in these types of battles," Kang suggests. "When you're in a war, a real-life human war, the good guys have to kill people. The so-called 'bad guys,' they're just trying to survive. Do the ends justify the means? *Star Wars* reaches into so much of the philosophy of survival and warfare."

That exploration of moral grayness is very much evident in *Cataclysm*, which tells an intense, breathtaking story pitting the Jedi against the Path of the Open Hand—essentially a cult with strong opinions about the Jedi's use of the Force.

"But it's interesting how if you take any

▶

07 08 Kang was inspired by her medical experience to write a 2-1B short story for *A Certain Point of View: The Empire Strikes Back* anthology.

09 Author Lydia Kang.

08

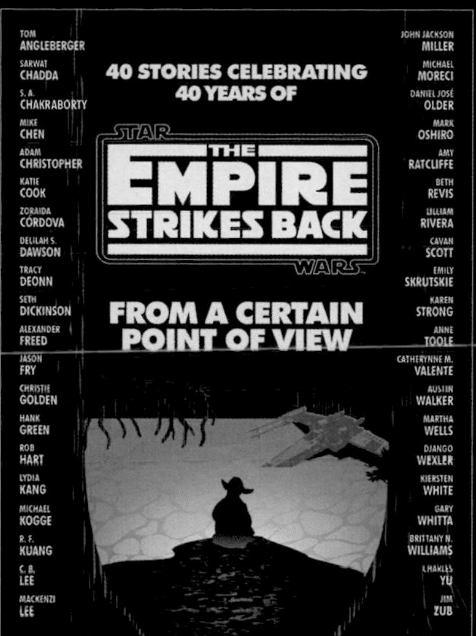

kind of belief system and you push it just so, and you twist it just so, it can turn into something that's really, really dangerous," Kang says. "And I love that sort of evolution shows up in Phase II."

Caught in the middle and being used as pawns in the Path's arsenal are the planets Eiram and E'ronoh, which have been stuck in a Forever War. The two planets may know how the war started, but they've forgotten the reasons why, Kang says. "Instead, their rulers and people continue to point fingers and try to prove their planet is more of a victim than the other.

It's a perspective war, and that's why it's not really clear who is good and who's bad," Kang explains. "That's why you see bad players show up on both sides. It's so ingrained in them both to win, no matter what the cost."

PURE MAGIC

Even though it is set in a galaxy far, far away, Kang suggests that *Star Wars* has become a cultural touchstone in the real world because it reflects our own humanity.

"There's so much of the human struggle in *Star Wars*, and the desires and hopes that we all have living our lives, every single day," Kang says, talking about how the saga treads a line between fantasy and real life, bridging intimate, personal stories with grand, galaxy-changing events. "It's because the focus is on these smaller stories, these really intimate relationships, while the perspective is on this big galactic scale," she says. "So, very much like in a fairy tale, you can cling onto these characters while there are all sorts of different magical and political things going on at the same time. Whatever you are going through, you can get through it with a beloved character. All the hardships, all the glory. And that's just pure magic."

09

Phase II: Quest Of The Jedi

Star Wars Insider revisits the key events of Phase II of Lucasfilm's *The High Republic* publishing initiative, with insight from authors Zoraida Córdova, Tessa Gratton, Claudia Gray, Lydia Kang, George Mann, Daniel José Older, and Cavan Scott.

WORDS: AREZOU AMIN AND CHRISTOPHER COOPER

Path of Deceit

Writers: Tessa Gratton and Justina Ireland
Disney Lucasfilm Press, Young Adult novel
A Force artifact has gone missing, and Padawan Kevmo Zink heads to Dalna with his master to investigate. There he meets and connects with Marda Ro, a member of the Path of the Open Hand, a group that believes the Jedi use the Force for ill.

"The Path of the Open Hand ultimately believes that the Force should be free—meaning, untouched," explains Tessa Gratton. "They believe using the Force at all causes unforeseen consequences and disrupts the balance of the galaxy. This puts them directly in opposition to the Jedi, and that was the original inspiration: exploring what kind of group would be philosophically the opposite of the Jedi, and then make it a dangerous cult with an even worse charlatan leader."

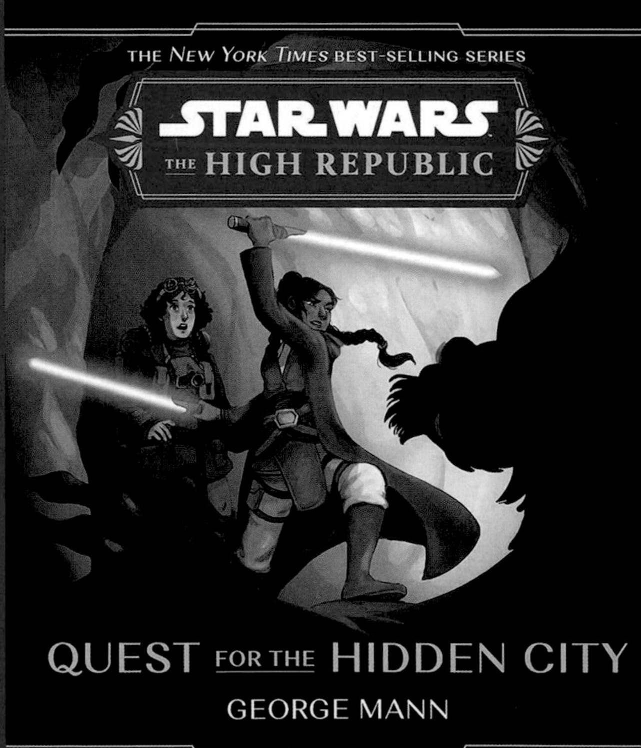

Quest for the Hidden City

Writer: George Mann
Disney Lucasfilm Press, Middle Grade novel
The Republic sends out Pathfinder teams to chart new courses in the Outer Rim and invite new worlds to join the Republic. When one team goes missing, Jedi Knight Silandra Sho and her Padawan Rooper head out to investigate on the haunted world of Gloam.

"The Pathfinders are small teams of Jedi, usually a master and a Padawan, and Republic citizens—a medic, a pilot, and a droid—brought together to explore the galactic frontier and make contact with the different worlds and beings they find living out there," says author George Mann. "They work with communications teams to establish a series of comms buoys, developing a larger communications network during a time when many hyperspace routes were yet to be discovered.

"This premise gave us the opportunity to show what the galaxy was like in the days before the Outer Rim had been fully explored, throwing our characters into all sorts of unexpected situations without the backup of Jedi or Republic forces," Mann continues. "With *Quest for the Hidden City*, I wanted to do a horror story for kids, with proper monsters and scares, but with a couple of important messages regarding the environment and the risks of ignoring the changing climate. Most of all, though, I wanted it to be fun!"

THE HIGH REPUBLIC: "TALES OF ENLIGHTENMENT"

Writer: George Mann

The Enlightenment tap bar on Jedha welcomes visitors with neither fear nor favor, and the regulars delight in the tales they bring with them.

"I loved writing about Enlightenment and the regulars that frequented it," George Mann enthuses. "I wanted to use each short story as a way of shedding light on a different aspect of what was happening on Jedha at that time, be it the conflict between Eiram and E'ronoh, or the different factions and sects at play in the Holy City. Alongside that, there was an opportunity to give Piralli and Moona their own story arcs, too. In The Battle of Jedha, Keth plays a fundamental part, while Piralli and Moona are his network of supporting characters. With the short stories there was a chance to discover how the major events of Phase II impacted them."

"New Prospects"
***Star Wars Insider* #213-#214**
Jedi Temple adjunct Keth Cerepath meets a down-on-her-luck prospector who recounts her harrowing encounter with pirates that led her to Jedha.

"A Different Perspective"
***Star Wars Insider* #215**
Keth Cerepath meets Whool, a member of the Path of the Open Hand who tells him about the Path's beliefs on the Jedi's abuses of the Force.

"The Unusual Suspect"
***Star Wars Insider* #216**
Enlightenment regulars Piralli and Moona fight back in their own way when a gang takes over their beloved tapbar.

"No Such Thing as a Bad Customer"
***Star Wars Insider* #217-#218**
Piralli and Moona help to defend Enlightenment when the Battle of Jedha reaches its doors.

"Last Orders"
***Star Wars Insider* #219**
Life returns to normal at Enlightenment, but it will never be quite the same.

Convergence

Writer: Zoraida Córdova
Random House Worlds, Adult novel
The worlds of Eiram and E'ronoh have been at war for years. The planets' heirs decide to marry to unite the worlds, but things go sour when the two are nearly assassinated. Jedi Gella Nattai and the chancellor's son Axel Greylark arrive to oversee the Jedi and Republic's interests but get swept up in a deadly conspiracy.

"*Star Wars* is a love story. Yes, it's about many other things—good, evil, politics, cute aliens, and funny droids, but we wouldn't have any of it without Padmé and Anakin's romance," suggests Zoraida Córdova. "Everything is the fallout from that romance. It was so epic it shaped the fate and fabric of the galaxy, and I kept that in mind while writing *Convergence*.

The heirs of Eiram and E'ronoh are symbolic of what we are capable of when people come together in friendship and kindness and partnership. But how committed to your duty and world do you have to be to show that by binding yourself to another person? Phan-tu and Xiri's choice signals to a tumultuous galaxy that they are committed to peace. Once that happens, they have to do the scariest thing—place their trust in someone else."

"THE BLADE"

Writer: Charles Soule,
Artists: Marco Castiello, Jim Charlampidis, Jethro Morales, and Jim Campbell
Marvel Comics
Four-issue mini-series

Jedi Knight Porter Engle, known as the Blade of Bardotta due to his extraordinary skills with a lightsaber, travels the galaxy with his sister Barash Silvain. On the planet Gansevor, their involvement in a local conflict threatens to change them both forever.

The four-issue mini-series "The Blade" fills in the backstory for Porter Engle, the Jedi Knight Soule created for Phase I. "Porter Engle is one of my all-time favorite creations," the comic-book writer has said.

The Battle of Jedha

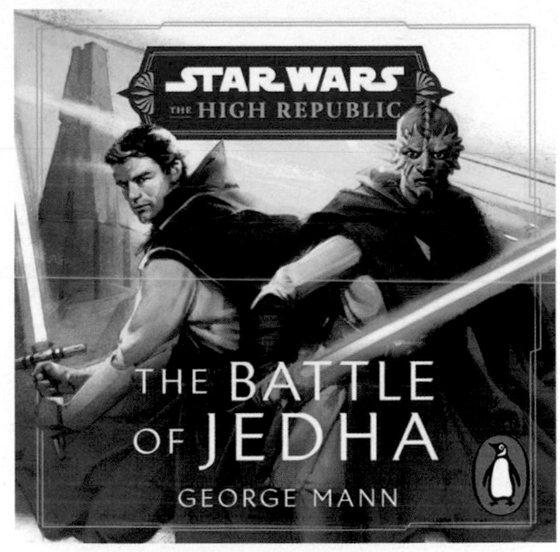

Writer: George Mann
Random House Worlds,
Audio Original novel

"The Forever War" between Eiram and E'ronoh has ended, and representatives from the planets meet on Jedha to sign a peace treaty, but tensions between different sects of Force users and worshippers are running high. Meanwhile, the Mother puts her own schemes into motion.

"Jedha at the time of the High Republic is no longer a Jedi stronghold and hasn't been for some time," explains George Mann. "They don't even have a temple there anymore. They're just one of the Force sects that hold the place sacred, and that was a really interesting angle for me. It gave us the opportunity to explore the Jedi through the eyes of other Force users and sects. Some of them welcomed the Jedi, some of them hated them, but most were ambivalent. That's an interesting melting pot to throw a handful of Jedi into.

"I always tell people that audio is a collaborative medium in a way that a novel isn't," Mann adds. "With an audio drama you're writing for the actors, not the end reader. You need to leave room for the actors to interpret the characters and lines as they see fit, and the end result is always a surprise, because it comes out sounding different—and usually far better—than it did in your imagination."

STAR WARS: THE HIGH REPUBLIC

Writer: Cavan Scott,
Artists: Ario Anindito, Andrea Broccardo, Mark Morales, Frank William, and Marika Cresta
Marvel Comics, 10 issues
Collected in two trade paperbacks.

Keeve Trennis becomes a Jedi Knight just as the peace of the High Republic is shattered by a series of deadly events.

Jedi Vildar Mac arrives on Jedha, just as the fragile peace begins to fall apart, and tensions run high between different factions, sweeping him and Padawan Matthea Cathley into a growing mystery.

"I'm always fascinated by people's relationship to their faith, and the Force is no exception," reveals Cavan Scott. "Jedha has enthralled me since *Rogue One: A Star Wars Story*. You can feel the history of the place, and easily imagine the kind of arguments that broke out between people with different belief systems. Phase II offered us a great chance to explore that."

"BALANCE OF THE FORCE" Issues 1-5
Vildar Mac and Matthea Cathley are drawn into a mystery on Jedha as tensions between different Force-worshipping factions begin to rise, Jedi are left for dead, and ancient relics begin to go missing.

"BATTLE FOR THE FORCE" Issues 6-10
During the Battle of Jedha, Vildar Mac is haunted by his past in a way that could spell his end, while Matthea Cathley and the thief Tey Sirrek continue the fight. Things go from bad to worse for the Jedi, all while the Leveler lurks in the shadows waiting to strike.

The High Republic: Tales of Light and Life

Writers: Zoraida Córdova, Tessa Gratton, Claudia Gray, Justina Ireland, Lydia Kang, George Mann, Daniel José Older, Cavan Scott, Charles Soule, and Alyssa Wong
Random House Worlds, Young Adult short-story collection

This short-story anthology gathers tales by each of the authors currently involved in Project Luminous. The stories are set in Phase I, II, and towards the beginning on Phase III, and follow the exploits of *The High Republic*'s heroes and villains, Jedi and Nihil, and everyone in between.

"This anthology was always intended to celebrate the entirety of *The High Republic*, with stories from each of our authors that will lead readers through every Phase of the initiative," says Lucasfilm Publishing creative director Michael Siglain.

"We have stories that are set before the events of *Convergence*, stories that are set post-*Path of Vengeance*, and stories that take place immediately following the fall of Starlight Beacon, with plenty of tales in between," he continues. "We're trying to give readers a wide variety of stories that focus on some of their favorite—and maybe soon-to-be-favorite—characters, while at the same time giving them stories of hope, love, horror, and friendship. There's something for everyone in *Tales of Light and Life*!"

Quest for Planet X

Writer: Tessa Gratton
Disney Lucasfilm Press, Middle Grade novel

A contest is announced to chart new hyperspace lanes, and hyperspace prospector Dass Leffbruk teams up with pilot Sky Graf and Padawan Rooper Nitani to find the mysterious Planet X. Unfortunately for the three teens, an encounter with the Path of the Open Hand drags them into the conflict between that group and the Jedi.

"Cavan Scott, Lydia Kang, and I had so many phone calls to work out how to weave the climaxes of our books together, since they all touch on the Night of Sorrow," says writer Tessa Gratton. "I probably had the easiest time, because Planet X was never intended to be directly involved in the battle itself. Once I knew what they were setting up, I worked out a way for my characters to help out the Jedi as part of their greater story, and what they needed from the Planet X plot to make it exciting and satisfying on its own."

STAR WARS: THE HIGH REPUBLIC ADVENTURES

Writer: Daniel José Older,
Artists: Toni Bruno, Michael Atiyeh
Dark Horse Comics, eight issues
Collected in two trade paperbacks.

Padawan Sav Malagan questions her life with the Jedi, as a chance encounter makes her contemplate the exciting life of space piracy.

"I was really excited at the idea of drawing a stark contrast to the Phase I adventures," says comic scribe Daniel José Older. "Sav's journey is, in many ways, a direct opposite of Lula's, who started out wanting to be the best Jedi ever and ended up unsure if she'd even be Knighted. I felt Sav should begin from a place of disillusionment with the Order. I wanted to tell a story about someone gifted and powerful who doesn't feel like the institution she's in lets her grow the way she needs to. Ultimately, I found a playful, complicated journey for Sav to go on, finding her way in the galaxy, in the Order, and most of all within herself."

VOLUME 1 Issues 1-4
Padawan Sav Malagan finds herself caught up in the adventures of space pirate captain Maz Kanata. As she gets to know Maz's crew, and gets involved in their hijinx, she starts to question whether this is the life she wants, or if she should return to the Temple to continue her training.

VOLUME 2 Issues 5-8
Sav Malagan and her new pirate friends embed themselves within the gang of marauders known as the Dank Graks and must work together to save Maz Kanata from the clutches of their leader Arkik Von.

THE EDGE OF BALANCE: PRECEDENT

Writers: Daniel José Older, Tomio Ogata Artist: Tomio Ogata
Viz Media

Wookiee Jedi Knight Arkoff joins the Battle of Dalna, helping the Jedi in their fight against the Path of the Open Hand. There, Arkoff's friend and former Padawan Azlin Rell falls victim to a terrifying new threat, one that may just tie into the Jedi's fight against the Nihil a century later.

"It was such a pleasure working on this story," Daniel José Older confirms. "The editorial team at Viz was great about guiding the voice and vibe and rhythm of the story to fit the manga aesthetic. Although I am a huge manga fan, they are the real experts. What was so much fun was bringing them a story and then getting to take part so actively in how it came to life. Shima Shinya, Mizuki Sakakibara, and Tomio Ogata were all dream-come-true collaborators—so creative and thoughtful with their contributions to story and art."

Cataclysm

Writer: Lydia Kang
Random House Worlds, Adult novel
Following the failed signing of the peace treaty, and thanks to the involvement of the Path of the Open Hand, violence has broken out once again between Eiram and E'ronoh. Out of options, Jedi Gella Nattai turns to Axel Greylark, now locked away in prison, for help in rooting out the cause of the renewed violence.

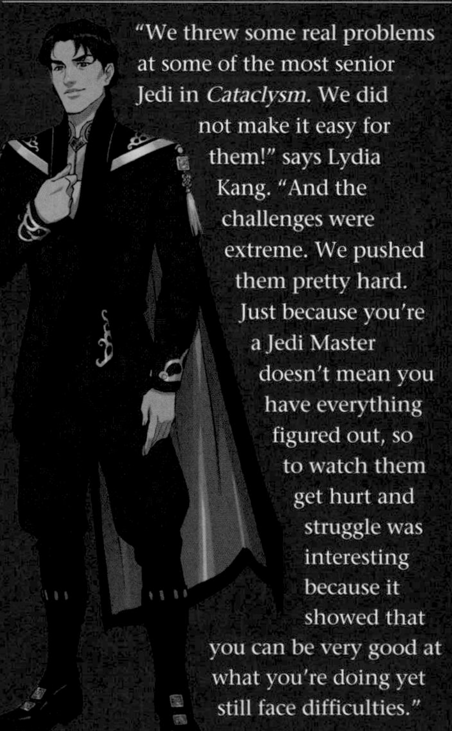

"We threw some real problems at some of the most senior Jedi in *Cataclysm*. We did not make it easy for them!" says Lydia Kang. "And the challenges were extreme. We pushed them pretty hard. Just because you're a Jedi Master doesn't mean you have everything figured out, so to watch them get hurt and struggle was interesting because it showed that you can be very good at what you're doing yet still face difficulties."

THE NAMELESS TERROR

Writer: George Mann,
Artists: Eduardo Mello,
Ornella Savarese
Dark Horse Comics
Four-issue mini-series

In the golden age of galactic exploration, the Jedi roam the galaxy on missions of discovery. When a team of Jedi encounter problems en route to Dalna, they are beset by both the dogmatic Path of the Open Hand, as well as a new uknown threat... a Nameless Terror.

"The Nameless are the embodiment of fear, in a way that only a Jedi can experience it. They're hunters, out to feast on the Living Force. Even being close to one can drive a Jedi to their knees. They're the answer to that initial question posed by the original five architects of *The High Republic*: What scares the Jedi? But that's all I can say for now..." confides George Mann, mysteriously.

QUEST OF THE JEDI

Writer: Claudia Gray,
Artists: Fico Ossio,
Sebastian Cheng
Dark Horse Comics
One-shot

In search of an ancient artifact, Jedi Knight Barnabus Vim and his Padawan Vix Fonnic arrive on Angcord. When they find the mysterious Echo Stone, they soon realize the fate of both the artifact and the people of Angcord may be closely tied.

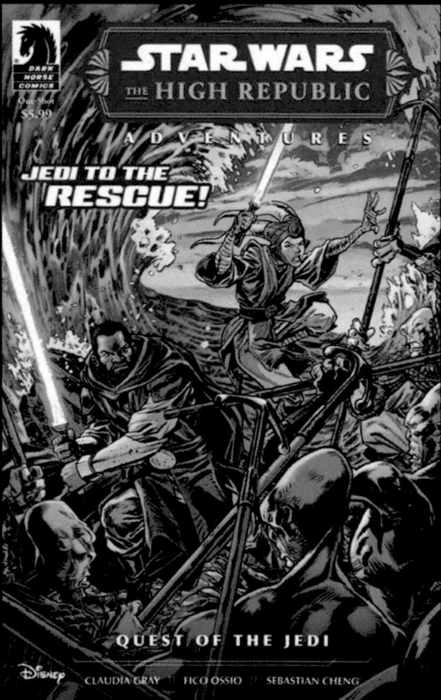

"The role of the Force in *Quest of the Jedi* didn't feel like a huge shift from what we've seen before—premonitions, metaphorical visions, an artifact with its own connection to the Force..." says Claudia Gray. "But my goal was to portray all this in a grand, hopefully somewhat Arthurian sense. The High Republic is itself a time of legend; their legends should have the feel of myth. So, it was less about doing something new as it was about showing the Force in a slightly different kind of storytelling tradition."

Path of Vengeance

Writer: Cavan Scott
Disney Lucasfilm Press, Young Adult novel
Cousins and Path of the Open Hand members Marda and Yana Ro are at an impasse, with Marda searching for Planet X and more creatures the Mother can use against the Jedi, while Yana tries to find a way to take control of the Path away from the Mother once and for all.

"It was a challenge to bring together so many different threads that had been laid out over Phase II," says Cavan Scott. "Justina Ireland and Tessa Gratton did such a great job setting up the Path in *Path of Deceit* that I always knew where I wanted to take them, delving deeper into how cult leaders manipulate and radicalize their acolytes."

Chronological Reader's Guide

PHASE I: LIGHT OF THE JEDI

Light of the Jedi
Writer: Charles Soule
Publisher: Del Rey
Release date: Jan 5, 2021

The Great Jedi Rescue
Writer: Cavan Scott
Publisher: Disney Lucasfilm Press
Release date: Jan 5, 2021
* *Note that this story takes place concurrent with* Light of the Jedi.

Into the Dark
Writer: Claudia Gray
Publisher: Disney Lucasfilm Press
Release date: Feb 2, 2021
**Note that this story takes place concurrent with* Light of the Jedi.

Star Wars: The High Republic Adventures (Ongoing Series)
Writer: Daniel José Older
Artist: Harvey Tolibao
Publisher: IDW Publishing
Release date: February 3, 2021

A Test of Courage
Writer: Justina Ireland
Publisher: Disney Lucasfilm Press
Release date: Jan 5, 2021

Star Wars: The High Republic (Ongoing Series)
Writer: Cavan Scott
Artist: Ario Anindito
Publisher: Marvel
Release date: Sep 7, 2021
**Note that while this story begins after the events of* A Test of Courage, *subsequent issues take place throughout* The High Republic.

The High Republic Adventures: The Monster of Temple Peak (Limited Series)
Writer: Cavan Scott
Artist: Rachel Stott
Publisher: IDW Publishing
Release date: Aug 11, 2021

The Edge of Balance, Vol. 1
Writers: Shima Shinya and Justina Ireland
Artist: Mizuki Sakakibara
Publisher: VIZ Media
Release date: Sep 7, 2021

The Rising Storm
Writer: Cavan Scott
Publisher: Del Rey
Release date: Jun 29, 2021

Showdown at the Fair
Writer: George Mann
Publisher: Disney Lucasfilm Press
Release date: Oct 5, 2021
**Note that this story takes place concurrent with* The Rising Storm.

Race to Crashpoint Tower
Writer: Daniel José Older
Publisher: Del Rey
Release date: Jun 29, 2021
**Note that this story takes place concurrent with* The Rising Storm.

Trail of Shadows (5-Issue Miniseries)
Writer: Daniel José Older
Artist: David Wachter
Publisher: Marvel
Release date: Oct 13, 2021

Out of the Shadows
Writer: Justina Ireland
Publisher: Disney Lucasfilm Press
Release date: Jul 27, 2021
**Note that this story takes place concurrent with* The Rising Storm.

Tempest Runner (Audiobook Original)
Writer: Cavan Scott
Publisher: Del Rey
Release date: Aug 31, 2021

Mission to Disaster
Writer: Justina Ireland
Publisher: Disney Lucasfilm Press
Release date: Jan 4, 2022

The Fallen Star
Writer: Claudia Gray
Publisher: Del Rey
Release date: Jan 4, 2022

PHASE I

Midnight Horizon
Writer: Daniel José Older
Publisher: Disney Lucasfilm Press
Release date: Feb 2, 2022
**Note that this story takes place concurrent with* The Fallen Star.

The Battle for Starlight
Writer: George Mann
Publisher: Disney Lucasfilm Press
Release date: Feb 2, 2022

The Edge of Balance, Vol. 2
Writers: Shima Shinya and Daniel José Older
Artist: Mizuki Sakakibara
Publisher: VIZ Media
Release date: Feb 22, 2022

Eye of the Storm (2-Issue Miniseries)
Writer: Charles Soule
Artist: Guillermo Sanna
Publisher: Marvel
Release date: Jan 12, 2022

PHASE II: QUEST OF THE JEDI

Quest for the Hidden City
Writer: George Mann
Publisher: Disney Lucasfilm Press
Release date: Nov 1, 2022

Path of Deceit
Writer: Justina Ireland and Tessa Gratton
Publisher: Disney Lucasfilm Press
Release date: Oct 4, 2022

Convergence
Writer: Zoraida Córdova
Publisher: Del Rey
Release date: Nov 22, 2022

Star Wars: The High Republic Adventures (Ongoing Series)
Writer: Daniel José Older
Artist: Toni Bruno
Publisher: Dark Horse
Release date: Nov 30, 2022

Star Wars: The High Republic (Ongoing Series)
Writer: Cavan Scott
Artist: Ario Anindito
Publisher: Marvel
Release date: Oct 12, 2022

Star Wars: The High Republic - The Blade (Miniseries)
Writer: Charles Soule
Artist: Marco Castiello
Publisher: Marvel
Release date: Dec 28, 2022

The Battle of Jedha (Audio Drama)
Writers: George Mann
Publisher: Random House
Release date: Jan 3, 2023 (audio only);
Feb 14, 2023 (script)

Quest of the Jedi
Writer: Claudia Gray
Artist: Fico Ossio
Publisher: Dark Horse
Release date: Mar 1, 2023

Quest for Planet X
Writer: Tessa Gratton
Publisher: Disney Lucasfilm Press
Release date: Apr 4, 2023

The Nameless Terror (Miniseries)
Writer: George Mann
Artist: Eduardo Mello and Urnella Savarese
Publisher: Dark Horse
Release date: Feb 22, 2023

Cataclysm
Writer: Lydia Kang
Publisher: Del Rey
Release date: Apr 4, 2023

Path of Vengeance
Writer: Cavan Scott
Publisher: Disney Lucasfilm Press
Release date: May 2, 2023